"A strange, origin[al]  in a mountain res[ort] and nightmares. Jonathan Harper writes nimbly, observes well, and imagines wildly. This is a terrific first novel."

Christopher Bram Lambda Literary Award-winning author of
Lives of the Circus Animals

"You Don't Belong Here reads like a Cheever fever dream—grim, literary, domestically harrowing. As far as narratives of alcohol go, Harper's book is a chilling revision of The Lost Weekend for a modern era."

L.A. Fields Lambda Literary Award finalist and author of
Homo Superiors

"You Don't Belong Here blends the finely wrought horror of a top-tier episode of the Twilight Zone with the observational deftness of Mary Gaitskill ... Through a tale that is equally terrifying and seductive, Harper captures the highly specific pain of a life unlived with an unflinching eye and a sharp humor."

Laura Bogart author of
Don't You Know I Love You

"Jonathan Harper has written a tight, tense novel that grabs you and doesn't let go. His lead character, a writer ending his residency in an artists' colony, finds himself trapped in an idyllic village which becomes decidedly less idyllic as he's stranded by his own self-sabotage and the treachery and manipulation of a shady cast of characters. Jonathan Harper has a fine eye for the damaged people who populate this village and this book, and sprinkles in enough dark humor to break the tension and give the reader an opportunity to breathe."

Rob Byrnes, Lambda Literary Award-winning author of
When the Stars Come Out

"This literary novel bursts at the seams with humanity."
Independent Book Reviews

Published by Lethe Press
lethepressbooks.com

Copyright © 2023 Jonathan Harper
ISBN: 978-1-59021-585-2

Cover Design & Typesetting: Ryan Vance

No part of this work may be reproduced or utilized in any form or by any means, electronic or mechanical, including photocopying, microfilm, and recording, or by any information storage and retrieval system, without permission in writing from the Author or Publisher.

This work is fiction, and any resemblance to any real person, dead or otherwise, is incidental

YOU DON'T BELONG HERE

Jonathan Harper

In loving memory
of Richard McCann

"The blurred world seen from a merry-go-round settled into place; the merry-go-round suddenly stopped."

> F. Scott Fitzgerald,
> *On Booze*

Chapter 1

The Public House took up the middle level of a crumbling stone building with long floorboards that creaked and a balcony so narrow one could easily fall to their death if they weren't careful. It was accessed by a wrought iron staircase that led to an unmarked door lit by a single sconce lantern. There was no sign, no advertisement, nothing to indicate the door held secrets. Because of this, the Public House seemed like an odd name for the bar, but then the Public House was an odd place. Road sign murals covered the walls, juxtaposed against the vacant stares of mounted deer heads. Tattered couches were spread among pedestal tables, and a chrome jukebox competed with an air conditioning unit that sputtered out the noise of farting bees; along the ceiling were strings of fairy lights that illuminated the bends and twirls of cigarette smoke. God willing, you could still smoke in a place like this.

Morris discovered the Public House on his last night in town and fell instantly under its spell. After one sip of beer, the room turned ghost-lit and conjured a premonition: the walls began to crumble as the floorboards shook loose, and he was swallowed up and fell towards the street below as the building collapsed on top of him. Then, the vision abruptly ended. And yet, whatever mountain magic had taken hold of him, it was not the malicious kind. There was no overwhelming dread or fear. All he felt was peace as if this was an ideal place and time to die.

"Morris?"

He thought he heard his name uttered in the crowd. Giving a quick glance back, he saw many faces but recognized none. Of course, it was silly to look at all. He was too far away from home, too far off the map; he knew no one here, and no one had reason to look for him. After another glance, he refocused on the blond woman sitting at his side. They had been chatting for a while now, and though she was not his type, she was interesting and possessed that rugged beauty he associated with Midwesterners. The overtures were obvious. She smoked Parliament after Parliament, tilting her head back and giving a throaty laugh at nearly everything he said. When her hand gently brushed against his wrist, he thought *No. I shouldn't.* He had not come out looking for an affair, but it was fun to think they were still possible.

"Morris."

This time, it was clear and unambiguous. As he turned, he found himself face-to-face with a short, pudgy man reaching out to tap his shoulder. From a distance, the stranger might have looked young, if not boyish. But up close, he was unnaturally weathered: round cheeks speckled with sunspots, crinkles around the eyes, his hair a tangled crow's nest. He grinned impishly as if on the verge of telling a crude joke.

"It's you. Isn't it?" the stranger asked.

When you stumble upon someone from your past, who do you want it to be? Who do you fear running into the most? Are they ever the same person? If Morris had been asked these questions, he wouldn't have had an answer. Until now—now when it stood in front of him as if it had always been there, constantly lurking in the periphery, grifting off whatever emotional residue was left.

Henry. The answer had always been Henry.

Christ Almighty, Morris thought, as if invoking divine protection against him.

"Fucking Moreece." Henry let the last syllable extend into a hiss as he waved his empty glass toward the bartender.

At one time, Henry had been beautiful, not handsome, but a beautiful boy: a cherub's head complete with freckles and loud eyes that gobbled up his face, all under a mass of curly brown locks. Back then, every gesture, every turn of the head was carefully choreographed to be almost toy-like. He had been as soft as a child's stuffed animal, the kind that said the most ridiculous things when you yanked his string.

He had still looked that way the last time they saw each other. It happened outside the Dupont Circle metro station during the blunt heat of summer, the kind of day that melted the good will off of commuters. As usual,

Morris was a mess: disheveled and sweating and probably muttering to himself. Whenever he was going, he was late. And then, in a single bitter moment, the world focused sharply on the figure approaching him: Henry, looking quite comfortable in his tank top and jean shorts, the bounce in his step showing he was in no hurry. Morris remembered it happening in slow motion, the way their eyes met, how Henry's face tilted towards him, both quizzical and apprehensive until they passed each other in silence. Just when he thought the moment was over, Morris heard the laugh, a stifled laugh, the mocking kind, and it took all of his energy not to turn around.

That was a decade ago when they both were different sorts of creatures.

The Henry standing in front of him now was a shadow of his former self, a piece of tarnished silver, a muddied boot, something life had dirtied up. The cherub's face was gone and replaced with coarse skin and puffy eyes; he was thicker in the gut. Morris had often wondered what would become of Henry when he finally lost his beauty.

They held each other's gaze for so long that Morris realized he nearly forgot about his lady friend. Her hand hovered close as if waiting for the right moment to pull him back. She cleared her throat. "So, I take it you two know each other?"

Henry turned and hissed, an openmouthed cat hiss that sounded even more ridiculous coming from a grown man. The woman blanched and scowled and could foresee their long history beginning to unravel; she knew she wanted nothing to do with it.

"Goodnight," she whispered to Morris and scurried off.

With her gone, they idled uncomfortably as Henry lit a cigarette. "Still equal opportunity, I see."

Say something, Morris told himself. *Ignore that last comment. But don't sit here gawking.* But there were no words, just a vacancy of rational thought. They had been friends once, wicked ones, but almost brotherly.

"And Yasmin?" Henry asked.

"We're engaged now," Morris said. "She says hi." *Of all the stupid things to say.*

"So, how'd you find me?"

His smile was triumphant as if he were the prize at the end of a scavenger hunt; the sight of it alone was exhausting.

"I wasn't looking for you. I'm at Manderlay... the artist colony up the road. I actually leave tomorrow..."

The grin vanished from his face. "I know what Manderlay is."

The bartender returned and set down his rocks glass with an audible thud. As Henry reached for it, his shirtsleeve pulled up, and Morris saw the scars. They snaked along the side of Henry's hand, along the wrist, and further up where his sleeve still partially concealed them: burn marks, deep pink and raw with ridges of hard white flesh that bubbled over and never settled. Whatever happened must have been painful.

"Should I buy you a drink?" Henry asked. "I'd like to, but I don't have any money."

He was an ugly man now, short and scarred and tired looking. Not ugly at first glance, but ugly by comparison and certainly ugly enough to know better than to play the same games he did in his youth. Still, Morris handed over a ten-dollar bill, and the bartender returned with a complimentary beer as a prize.

"Well, that was nice of you," Henry said. He flung his scarf over his shoulder in a dramatic gesture that was half-dismissive and half-beckoning before he wandered away as abruptly as he arrived.

Whatever spell had fallen over him quickly faded as Morris felt that familiar soreness of old grudges. Their friendship had ended badly and left an emotional bruise that had ached for years. He used to fantasize about running into Henry again and had rehearsed every biting truth he would say, but now that it finally happened, he was surprised at how ill-prepared he was.

And yet, Morris found himself following Henry across the bar, clutching his beer like a weapon, as ghastly anxiety grew in his belly. He knew this sensation well. He was wandering into the tunnel. *The* Tunnel. An old private joke from their college days, something you said to goad an unwilling participant into action. The Tunnel wasn't long, but it zig-zagged its way through the circles of drinkers until it had led him to the back end of the Public House.

Henry stood with a small cluster of men hovered around a pedestal table and as Morris approached, they all went silent. There were five men in total, older, all grizzly and grim, wearing the tell-tale signs of sweat and labor, vanguards of some forgotten code. They quietly appraised him as if trying to guess the value of a trinket in a store window. All except Henry, who whispered into one of their ears, smiling evilly as he did it. Morris felt his anxiety peak and wondered if he'd been lured into a den of wolves.

"Are you gonna introduce us to your friend? Or are ya just being rude?" This came from the tall man on the opposite side of the table. His voice was a low murky pitch, yet it cut through the white noise of the bar and demanded attention. Everything about the tall man demanded attention.

To this, Henry tensed up, eyes wide as eggs, and began to stutter.

"You really are a pissant sometimes," the tall man said. He crossed over and shook Morris's hand in a tight grip. The tall man was billowy and broad, his face acne-scarred with trimmed muttonchops. "New blood," the tall man said. "We could use some new blood." There was a gluttonous look in his dark red mouth. It was impossible to look at such a mouth and not think, *This man eats meat.*

The rest of the table gave a few nods and grunts and resumed their conversations.

Thank God there was no room for him to sit, else he'd fit in snugly, shoulder-to-shoulder with them. To his left, Henry stared over the rim of his glass. There was evil in his eyes as if he were plotting mischief but hadn't quite decided what that mischief should look like. To his right, the tall man loomed and raked his fingers through his mutton chops. Morris sipped his beer cautiously and then felt with nauseating conviction that it was his turn to speak.

"I'm at the Manderlay Colony," he finally said and watched the tall man's eyebrow lift as if to say *Oh, one of those.* A dry moment went by, and then nothing. He wet it down with another sip of beer. Usually, there was the song and dance of being asked about his projects and delaying his response to prove he was not too eager to tell. Not tonight. They were probably used to the trickle of artists and writers and other visiting eccentrics.

"Tonight's his last night," Henry said.

"Unfortunately," Morris added.

"I see. Out for one last fling before you go." The man's red mouth curved into something wicked as they clinked their beer bottles together with a little ting.

"I'm sure Yasmin won't mind," Henry interjected.

Oh, the bitch! To reference Yasmin, to act like she was an ace hidden up his sleeve. Henry had no right to evoke her name, much less assume anything about what she minded. Morris went hot under the collar, and felt that fiery urge to lash out. But that's what Henry liked. Reactions, raw dramatic reactions.

Instead, Morris looked for ways to extradite her from the conversation and retreated to another benign topic. "What do you do here?" he asked and the tall man scoffed. Instead, they mulled over the town and the end of tourist season and the long winter that would follow. New blood, the tall man said again. This town needs more new blood to keep it interesting. The words dripped from his mouth. Then, Morris turned back to Henry. "And what do you do?" he asked sweetly.

"I live," Henry said. He was starting to look annoyed.

"Well damn, you're rude tonight," the tall man quipped as he downed his beer. "Must be the thirst talkin'. Go get us another round."

"But I'm not done with mine yet." At first, Henry's voice held a defiant little spark, but it quickly extinguished. He downed the rest of his glass in a single gulp and his gnarled hand once again came into plain view. The burns were even more grotesque this time around, the skin having puckered up with the tenderness of raw meat as if the slightest touch might cause the wounds to reopen.

"Go on now," the tall man said and forced a wad of crumpled bills into Henry's greedy fingers. There was another moment of hesitation, and then the tall man's thick hand swooped in and grabbed Morris's side, pulling him close. "Don't worry," he said. "We'll keep your friend company."

With that, Henry retreated into the crowd.

They were alone now, surrounded by countless swaying bodies, people laughing and choking on cigarettes, drunkards telling stories or trying to sing along to the music. As Morris stood there, he felt the grip around his waist tighten as he sank deeper into the thick body next to him. It radiated with heat and musk and sweat, that bestial combination. He felt snuggled up to a wild animal, one that could turn violent at any sudden movement. The paw gripped his side harder and began to palpitate; he gently wiggled away.

"Where are you going?" the tall man asked.

"It's getting late. I got an early flight tomorrow."

Morris gave him a coy smile. He was in the Tunnel now. Deep in it. The Tunnel was where you ended up when you were feeling uncertain and tempted, when you were teetering a line.

"Hold on. Your drink's coming and you got so many more people to meet. Like Jack, here." The tall man pulled in one of the other men from the table, a swollen man with demure shoulders and fleshy breasts that he kept covering with his arms. His face was scrunched together in such a way to appear too small for his head.

"Nice to meet you," Jack said in a wistful voice.

"Speak up. Tell him where you're from."

"Tulsa," Jack said. The word came out slow and wounded.

"Yup, we stole the best short-order cook from Tulsa," the tall man said. "Jack came to us about nine or ten years ago and loved it so much, he never left." He continued for a few moments, giving Jack's unremarkable biography, a life confined to a rented shack, a flatiron grill, and a collection of action figures that no child would recognize. It was pitiful, or at least made to sound pitiful, as if his loneliness was something that could be disassembled and put on display piece by piece. "If you're ever in need of inspiration, just gaze upon good old Jack here."

"Please stop," Jack moaned. "I'm on the verge of tears."

"See what I mean?"

They were all relieved when Henry returned, balancing three rocks glasses and Jack was able to slink back into the shadows. Morris sniffed his drink, and it seared his nostrils; it was raw whiskey. No good would come from it. But the others had already toasted and were downing theirs without hesitation, so he did the same. The liquid burned and settled in his stomach and released a paroxysm of déjà vu. Suddenly, Morris could remember countless nights from their college years doing just this: loitering in smokey bars and letting strangers get them drunk, all while playing coy. He turned to Henry as if to say, *remember that time*, and tried to pluck out one of their many adventures to retell.

Suddenly, all the lights went out, and they were shrouded in darkness. The jukebox went silent and all conversations ceased, except for one shrill voice of a lady belting out the punch line of a joke. "No. We call him Porky because he likes to fuck pigs," she exclaimed with an exaggerated Southern twang. The bar erupted in laughter. Within moments, the darkness was cut by little beacons of glowing cellphones and the orange dots of lit cigarettes. A hand brushed against the side of his jeans and Morris moved away. Taking the opportunity, he moved through the shadowed crowd toward the exit. Yet, even in the dark, he could feel the tall man's gaze upon him, watching him go.

The bartender called out, "If you owe a tab, do not leave!"

She held up her phone like a lantern and Morris dodged the light as he stepped through the front door and ran down the metal staircase and embraced the street below. He was eager to leave the Public House behind him.

The whole town had succumbed to the blackout. Everything was dark. Every corner, every crevice. The sky was full of stars. He walked up the main street, passing storefront windows that looked like portals into the abyss and started to imagine the town had gone completely dead; he was the only man left alive. Buildings around him became cliffs and towers. He envisioned a hundred thousand pitfalls lay ahead of him. But soon signs of life disrupted the fantasy: the creaks of doors, and another pedestrian crossing the street ahead of him. Upward, hotel balconies were filling with people, smoking and whispering. Somewhere farther down, a woman screamed loudly and laughed at some pitch-black mishap.

Around the corner, a car came speeding down, howling in the night. The engine revved and boys hollered from its open windows and Morris shrieked as a bottle crashed near him as they soared by.

Fuck. That was meant for me. Morris slunk backward as if the bottle had shattered against his gut. And then, fearful the car might return, he dashed up the hill and into the neighborhoods until he was far away from the downtown and its petty anarchy. Still, he could not outrun the blackout. Through the dark, he turned off the main road until he found a bench to sit. As his eyes adjusted, he could make out the edge of a small fenced-in grotto bordered by two snuffed-out lampposts. The sculpture garden. He could see the shapes of figures within, large abstract bodies in various poses. In the moonlight, they were almost ethereal.

The town was full of these little spots—all hidden among the stone walkways and hills and Victorian gingerbread houses. Parts of the town were cut deeply into the mountainside with hidden grooves and stone-cut architecture. Somewhere, on the opposite ridge, was the imposing Jesus statue. He'd seen it his first day, the colossal structure that peered over downtown, arms stretched as if it held dominion. At first, the statue disturbed him. Over time, it was another detail to admire.

He had been in town a week, seven days that had dragged on and yet passed as quickly as water through a sieve. A week was enough time to orient oneself, to find a rhythm at the artist colony, to select a favorite drinking hole. It was enough time to feel settled, productive, and then restless. He had only begun to explore the town and there was still so much left to see. But now the week was over; it was time to go home.

The Manderlay Colony was Yasmin's idea. She had researched it, sitting at their dining table with her evening sherry, sifting through dozens of websites. She practically assembled the application herself, crafting his letter of intent, editing his writing samples, and calling her legions of artsy friends for reference letters. She even provided the funding. Yasmin was good like that; she was a doer, much savvier with money.

"I want you to do something," she told him. "Go have an adventure. Work on your book."

"It sounds like you're trying to get rid of me," he said, to which she rolled her eyes in exasperation. Wasn't she always bartering with him to do things, knowing full well he was perfectly content lounging around their apartment all day? They lived outside Washington, D.C.

and Yasmin often complained that he never went to the museums or the theater, ate at the same restaurants, and always saw the same people. A terrible thought occurred to him: this trip was necessary because she was getting bored of him; because he was now boring.

What would Yasmin say if she saw him now, huddled in the dark? *So, you just left?* He could mentally picture her standing beside him, exhaling an unnerving sigh as she dug through her purse for that hidden pack of smokes. *What happened tonight was a one-time act of divine intervention. You'll never have that opportunity again. You should have stayed. You should have talked to him. At least get some closure.*

There had been a time when their lives were so interlocked, when Yasmin, pragmatic stoic Yasmin, had doted on them as if caring for wounded little birds. Back then, Henry had been a central figure, a delicate dove in a cage who kept masochistically plucking out all its beautiful feathers. For better or worse, their world had once revolved around him.

As Morris sat there, he felt a sudden pang of regret. He regretted escaping the way he did as much as he wondered what exactly he had escaped from. The opportunity presented itself, and like a startled animal, he chose flight over fight, despite no present danger. And now, he was alone, tragically sober, with no one to talk to.

"It's been a rough few years, and money was tight, but I survived," he muttered as if Henry were right there next to him. "Still live in Virginia, still work at the newspaper, practically run the advertising department all on my own… but I'm finally getting back to writing for myself again… Remember all those stories we used to tell each other? All those ideas we had? I'm finally putting them down in a book. It's what we always talked about…"

Morris felt his throat seize up. A twinge of pure embarrassment shot through the self-pity. He wanted to tell Henry about his life, to wallow in that painful nostalgia for those nights when they had loitered in cafes for endless hours, talking about anything and everything. He wanted to feel sentimental and for it to hurt, if not emotionally scar, one of them or both. "I've missed you," he said aloud. "Even if you were an asshole." He knew how ridiculous he sounded. Thankfully, there was no one around to hear him.

The night dragged on in the sober quiet. It was half past eleven; he was ready for the comfort of a warm bed. There was a time in his life when they didn't dare show up to the party until nearly midnight.

Get up. Stop stalling.

It was another half-mile's walk back, past the sculpture garden and through the winding neighborhood of antique houses. Everything was dark and damp, the air uncharacteristically warm for October. Clawed fingers of weeds and bushes edged over the narrow walkways. Morris thought of snakes lashing out at his sandaled feet with every rustle.

The Manderlay Colony was accessed by a short bridge and two suspended walkways hovering over the hiking trails underneath. On the other side was a small parking court, flanked by a dozen brightly painted cottages and the converted barn that served as the communal kitchen.

It was eerily lit in the moonlight and quiet enough to hear the rustle of deer somewhere in the distance.

When he first arrived, he found the quiet disturbing. Both day and night, the entire colony rang with absolute silence as the other residents worked feverishly in their studios, occasionally sitting out on their patios to read. When he saw them, the most they would give was a polite nod of acknowledgment. On his first night, he made the mistake of streaming music from his laptop, which ended with a curt knocking on his door. People were trying to work, they told him.

By mid-week, he learned to love the quiet and the blank canvas it created in his mind. He happily spent hours pacing the interior of his studio, thinking out loud or humming to himself. There were the delirious nights alone on his patio, sipping whiskey from a plastic cup, a time reserved to think and feel. He had eased into the ways of the other residents until he was invited to join them for morning walks into town or to remain in the barn after dinner to drink wine and talk. There was the mystery writer who told too much gossip and the charming poet who described his meeting Allen Ginsberg as though it were his greatest accomplishment. His favorite was the collage artist, a pretty middle-aged woman who waltzed around covered in beaded jewelry and long hemp skirts. She spent half the year at similar residencies across the country. "In my humble opinion," she had said very matter-of-factly, "you come to these to get a little bit of work done but really to network and sleep around." Not that he received any invitations.

Still, it was a good week, a long week that had flowed gently at first until it evaporated in a puff of steam. It was a week of handwritten notes and world building and rereading sections of Tolkien and hovering over his laptop while furiously talking to himself. And now that it was over, there was still so much unfinished.

As he approached his cottage, he kept thinking, *just one more week*. Because if he wanted it hard enough, then it was his for the taking.

"Is that you, Morris?" It was Mrs. Oglesthorpe, the painter in the cottage next door. She was a rotund grandmotherly figure, a self-proclaimed watchdog against mischief, and an enforcer of rules. *All* of them. "What are you mumbling about? You're not drunk, are you?"

"No, it was nothing," he said. His mind was clear from the long walk back, but he was no longer in the mood for conversation. "Sorry if I disturbed you."

"Lights went out everywhere." She sat on her patio as if she'd waited up for him. "Kind of late to be trotting around in the dark. You should be more careful. Imagine if you had taken a tumble. No one would find you till sunrise."

"I was very careful," he assured her, fumbling with his keys.

She seemed to be on the verge of an interrogation. From the beginning, she'd been aware of his novice status and therefore monitored his every movement: timing her internal clock around his arrival to dinner to when his toilet flushed. The old lady could be everywhere without ever letting a foot drop beyond her patio.

"You have an early flight tomorrow. Make sure your rooms are cleaned up before you go."

"Yes, ma'am," he said and went inside before she could say anything else.

The cottage was a compact space with the efficiency of a Japanese bento box. The front room held a writing desk, bookcase, and a café table barely large enough to accommodate a visitor for tea. Just beyond were two separate areas: a washroom and a tight kitchenette. The bedroom was in the back, with three outward-facing windows that looked out upon the wooded ridge.

Of course, he'd made a mess of it all. As his eyes adjusted to the dark, he could see the wreckage: the clusters of beer cans, overflowing wastebaskets, and piled dishes in the sink next to the half-drunk bottle of Jack Daniels. He had taken the cottage and turned it into an alcoholic's dream of a writing den. Even his dirty clothes had migrated out all over the studio and created the illusion that he'd spent the majority of the week naked.

After a quick visit to the toilet, he stripped out of his smoky clothes and set the alarm on his phone, hoping there was enough battery left to survive the night. The fan didn't work, and it was unbearably warm; beads of sweat quickly turned into a pool against the mattress. He lay there, staring at the ceiling, hands creeping under his briefs, and gave a few soft tugs. His mind trailed through a roster of faces, Yasmin's first, and then to the various people at the bar, the blonde woman and the tall man, and finally, it settled on Henry. It felt like he had an erection at a funeral.

"You're an idiot," he muttered, still to Henry. "You look like shit, you know." And then, he fell into a trance, not quite sleep, not quite dream, but an unrestful mental tour of the various times and places they had shared.

He fell asleep wandering into the Tunnel.

Chapter 2

They called it the Tunnel. Or entering the Tunnel. Or falling into the Tunnel. It was a vague feeling of uncertainty, an unquantifiable notion of danger or consequence. When you were inside, that's when trips turned bad when you felt anxious and paranoid, when you could hear your conscience whispering: *Should I be here? Is this a good idea?*

Morris felt the Tunnel more acutely than others. While his friends carelessly drifted in and out, he would feel it coming on like a sneeze until he was overcome. The word "trespass" often burrowed into his mind with such force that it wiped out all other thoughts. That was how he often felt: like a trespasser in other people's lives.

One particular night out during their sophomore year, they were lumped together outside Badlands in a long line of club kids extending all the way to P Street.

"I'm done. Let's go someplace else," Morris said. "I don't even like this place."

"Trust me. It's really fun in there," Henry said, his hand poised on his hip in a dramatic arch. He wore a neon orange jumper with no shirt underneath and his sex pants, a pair of linen trousers with one of the pockets torn out so anyone could reach inside. He was more than ready.

When they finally entered, the cashier charged them ten dollars each and marked their hands with oppressive black Xs. Inside, the dance floor pulsed with the collective heartbeat of a hive, all droning and sweating. Almost instantly, Henry was absorbed into the writhing mass, and Morris found himself adrift. The music was dreadful, some epileptic version of an *NSYNC song that bled into a Britney song. The strobe lights made everyone indistinguishable from each other. There was a sidebar and plenty of alcoves, but those were off-putting as well. They were all full of scowling boys smoking their cigarettes and the men who stood watching with butcher's eyes, trying to determine what meat was the freshest. He was ready to leave when Henry rematerialized with two plastic cups and his impish smile.

It was Morris's opinion that places like this should be dark, the music atmospheric, and there should always be plenty of seating. He hated dancing; he was a terrible dancer. As he wandered the club in a state of wistful contempt, the Tunnel began to take hold. *I should not be here.* He dodged the occasional glance, certain that people were frowning at him. *This place is not for you*, the Tunnel reminded him. *These are not your people.*

A few drinks later, he needed to piss and was forced to navigate the club alone. The bathrooms were dimly lit and not too crowded, but while washing his hands, he became aware of a figure standing behind him. It was an older man, a muscular man with a militant square jaw and crew cut. His sneer was almost performative. Suddenly, Morris was clasped by both shoulders as the stranger leaned in and growled in his ear. "Call me *Sir*." In those sickening few seconds, he could feel his pulse twitch in every vein, but he said nothing. All he could do was stare through the mirror. And then it was over. "Forget it," the man grumbled and moved away.

Once the shock passed, Morris found himself oddly exhilarated by the experience. He wandered around in a dazed state, looking for the mysterious stranger, the word "sir" straddling the edge of his tongue. But the man was long gone, and as if sensing the loss of one of their own, the crowd grew increasingly more hostile. Everyone was scowling. They spilled drinks on his shoes and elbowed him for standing too close. A gyrating man practically flung a glowstick in his face before spiraling away.

Morris hated this club, and the act of keeping himself together was crushing his heart within him. He would be back again next week.

Two hours later, they were in a posh apartment on the other side of Dupont Circle. Henry lounged on the sofa, leg draped over their host's lap as he drank vodka from a crystal tumbler. The two huddled together, giggling at some inaudible joke between them. Morris stood fidgeting next to the other fellow, a short, brawny man, overdressed as if he'd come straight from the opera. "Let's go look at the moon," the man kept offering. It was the first night he let a stranger fondle his cock, out on the tiny balcony, a short-lived venture as Morris orgasmed after a few brief strokes. "Good for you," the man said and retreated inside. Below, drunken voices of late-night stragglers serenaded the streets as Morris tried to recall the exact chain of events that led him here.

The Tunnel was like that. You crept in, like a dare, and wondered how far you were willing to go.

They met at Marymount University in the back row of Dr. Cullinane's Intro to Western Philosophy course. For the entirety of that first semester, they existed on the periphery of each other, exchanging a few pleasant conversations, and sharing smokes during the class break, but mostly with Morris observing him from afar. Despite being a poor student, Henry appeared ironically knowing compared to Morris's other friends. He was exceptionally intelligent, a combination of being well-read and well-traveled that was quite unexpected in an eighteen-year-old. His weekly disruptions in class sent poor Dr. Cullinane fumbling for a response every time. And yet, after lectures, he never holed up in the library under a pile of books or, as Morris did, go disappointedly to his dorm room to study while dreaming of the adventures he might have if he were more brazen. No—Henry did the college a favor by dropping in for a few hours before disappearing into the bowels of DC each night.

Henry was always telling stories. One moment, he'd be happily discussing his latest obsession with Sarah McLaughlin or Sailor Moon and then abruptly transition into a wild tale of how a trip to the Hair Cuttery ended in a S&M bar and how he had to barter with a dominatrix for a ride home. Everything he said had an air of urgency to it, as if it were all prefaced with *Sit back, kids, this is going to be the most important thing you hear today.*

They were unlikely friends because Morris possessed a quiet, contemplative nature. He was an observer with a passive streak, tragically thin and unassuming. Because he had few stories to tell, he quickly fell out of Henry's range of vision until the following semester when they stumbled upon each other during those insomniac hours of the Metro 29 Diner. As Morris remembered it, he sat alone in his booth sipping 2 a.m. coffee, buried in a textbook, when Henry materialized out of nowhere and plopped across from him with the jubilance of finding a long-lost friend. Within seconds, he was gossiping as usual.

"The thing about Blair I can't stand is that she's a poser. Like, she's desperate for everyone to think she's this responsible voice of reason, and the minute other people are having more fun than her, she goes batshit crazy." Blair was another classmate from their philosophy course, a sarcastic girl with a mean streak. She had recently thrown a party at her new boyfriend's apartment. "Oh, it was awful," Henry was saying. "Half the night, she was showing off and complaining about how stressed she was. Like, we get it—you're sleeping with a law student, you're pre-med, you got a part-time job, and a hundred other things going on. Like, that's a lot of pressure. But you know, I think a lot of that pressure is self-induced.

She piles things up, so she's got an excuse to go nuts. All of a sudden, she announces she needs to lighten up and starts downing tequila shots. It was a mess."

As Morris listened, a strange affection manifested itself. He enjoyed listening to Henry analyze her, even if it was unkind. "I didn't even know Blair was dating anyone."

Henry gave him a befuddled look. "Really? Oh my God, you should call her. She'd love to hear from you."

Every week, they met at the diner and chained-smoked Marlboros and consumed endless cups of coffee. It was an intimate ritual, arriving around midnight and not leaving until near sunrise. They gossiped recklessly, but they discussed other things, too: their families and politics, the films they loved and hated, the philosophy of video games, and their mutual disdain for all things religious. One night, Morris rambled about the fantasy novels he consumed throughout high school. He was not sure why, but he was unable to stop talking. Perhaps the mix of caffeine and nostalgia created a most intoxicating elixir, and he was drunk off it. Within an hour, he had spiraled into an entire history of his childhood filled with fantasy worlds and then into the long-winded plots of novels he would one day write. He practically vomited all his nerdy musings onto the table for full display, only taking a breath to signal the waitress for another refill. He had an entire series of books all in his head but was waiting for the right time to commit them to paper. And then, after finishing his pitch for the stories, came the sudden drop. Henry was silent, head gently nodding.

He looked fatigued and in need of rescue. The horror quickly set in: Morris was embarrassing himself; all of this was embarrassing. Shortly after, they called it a night. And then came the grim realization that he had revealed too much, and their friendship was probably over. However, the next week, Henry arrived in his same bouncing manner, this time eager to add his own contributions to the stories.

It was during this time that Morris claimed they fell in love.

Throughout college, they were known as a joint package. There was an unwritten but widely accepted law: where you had one, the other was close by.

Morris dated loud girls, proud girls—ambitious, lionhearted ladies who tended to bully him. When the infatuation wore off, he softly retreated from their lives as the appropriate hour struck. His relationships worked on an internal clock, slowly ticking down to their expiration, and afterward, his ex-lovers regarded him politely.

Henry, on the other hand, didn't date. He simply fucked and was often fucked in return. His jaunts into DC were populated with a harem of older men, lovers, tricks, and dealers. He rotated among them, returning to the dorms the following day, sore and battle-scarred and happily willing to share every intimate detail of the night before.

Henry was also a very embarrassing boy. His eyes would light up with childish glee whenever he scored a horrified gasp from his audience. "I lost my virginity when I was thirteen," he'd say drolly, "to my father's friend. Best dinner party ever." He'd walk arm in arm with an uncomfortable-looking girl, mentioning how his asshole itched after too much sex or complaining about the poor performance of his latest partner. Once, he brought the entire dining hall to an abrupt silence. "I just don't understand," he said. "If you don't have a prostate, how does that feel good?"

He thought he was shocking and shocking people when he was only embarrassing them—and often himself.

Worrying about what someone thought of you was another sign you were stuck in the Tunnel. Henry and Morris floated this word between them on those nights out, which grew increasing and damaging in number. They evoked the Tunnel as though it were a dare.

There also was the danger of lingering in it for too long. That was when someone burned out or got phony or worse. Friends of theirs had been lost to it without ever knowing its name. The Tunnel's first victim was Blair, who crashed and burned until her parents pulled her out of college. There was Trent, who OD'd. And then Max, who went home one summer and returned as a born-again evangelist.

After graduation, they moved into a two-bedroom apartment in Fairfax, where the rents were still cheap. It was filled with hand-me-down furniture and pathetically decorated with little artifacts they had accumulated. A pair of dumpster-rescued bookcases held old textbooks, mounds of VHS tapes, and tiny wind-up toys. The walls were covered with Henry's posters of the Flaming Lips and Lars von Trier films, all set against the Moroccan-styled tapestry they purchased from Urban Outfitters. As if to complete the mix-and-matched décor, Morris added a small collection of glass jars he arranged along the kitchen bar. Their balcony remained empty except for two folding chairs with an old coffee tin serving as the ashtray. None of this mattered.

It was a good first year, a year financed by monthly checks from Henry's parents, a year of continued self-discovery, a year of house parties, clubbing, and spending time nursing hangovers in front of the TV. It was a year of desperate trips to the Whitman Walker Clinic and the awful waiting period for HIV tests, followed by relief and promises to be more careful. It was a year of odd jobs and internships to nowhere, as well as a year of too much free time. Countless nights were spent smoking on the balcony, fighting off the urge to sleep. When they ran out of things to talk about, they would return to mapping out the fantasy world they had started at the diner, always discarding the previous incarnations in favor of a fresh start. They read old *Forgotten Realms* novels and the *Sandman* comic books and analyzed the plots. And when the creative juices dried up, they consumed bowls of ramen or snorted lines of coke and discussed their eventual jobs.

"One day, you'll be running your own publishing house," Henry would say. "You'll have a Manhattan office and a line of fantasy authors as well as ghostwriters to finish your own series. You will have to proofread everything, and for every error, someone gets sacked!" Then, Henry's eyes would sparkle. "Now, tell me about my career!"

Sometimes, they took the Metro into DC and walked around the monuments at night, unmindful of the homeless. They paced along the Reflecting Pool, humming quietly to themselves until they reached the steps of the Lincoln Memorial. They sat at the Einstein statue, smoking under cover of the foliage, before moving along the government buildings. Sometimes they went to Henry's bars, where they were still young enough to procure free drinks from hopeful daddies. When he was having a dry spell or whatever girl he was seeing lost interest, Morris would allow himself to be beckoned into the bathroom by some authoritative man and come out glowing with delicious guilt.

Sometimes Henry went off alone, and when he did, he might disappear for days. On those nights, Morris wandered absentmindedly through the apartment: microwaving his dinner, talking to himself, watching an endless stream of late-night TV. It was strange to be alone. The apartment felt frozen in place and suddenly fragile as if the smallest vibration could make the walls crash down. And then, in the darkest hours, he could hear the front door open and Henry moving through the dark rooms, often discarding his clothes, perhaps showering, before he'd crawl into Morris's bed and curl up next to him.

Sometimes they had sex, but most times, they didn't. It became a little transaction between them, a "help me out" moment when there was an itch that needed scratching. They rarely discussed it except to instruct in what they liked. After all, there was no point in stretching it out longer than it needed to be.

With each month, the Tunnel expanded and contracted. There were periods when they were both gripped with uncertainty, a pale understanding that what they had was not sustainable. Quickly, they shrugged it off and basked in the glory of having no family, no schedule, not enough money, and a far, far away future. If the Tunnel taught them anything, it was that the current moment was everything.

In their second year, Morris took a job at a community newspaper and spent the first week debating whether or not to quit. The office was dismal and disorganized, a cocoon-like nest of compact desks, overstuffed boxes, loose papers, and abandoned Styrofoam cups. Dirty windows strained the sunlight into a puree of light, so one had the perception that they were bathing in soup. The rest of the staff seemed oblivious to their surroundings. They were a strange pack of aging hipsters who spent each weekday drinking and talking about local politics until they threw themselves into a panicked frenzy to produce the weekly edition. It was unclear how they managed, but a new paper was printed each Thursday morning, and the staff breathed a sigh of relief for surviving another week.

At first, he wondered how anyone could work in such a place, but it felt more and more appropriate over time. He liked his niche in the advertising department, throwing together sloppy ads in Photoshop and fitting them like puzzle pieces into the layouts. He took on the invoicing because no one else wanted the responsibility. It was dull, repetitive work, but there was satisfaction in instilling order onto chaos. He was also free to come and go as he pleased as long as the manifest was accurate and all the emails were answered. After a few short months, he felt like he had finally excelled at something.

For reasons he couldn't quite understand, this hurt Henry's feelings. Any mention of the newspaper, no matter how trivial, annoyed him. "You're always talking about work," Henry complained but never offered a new topic of conversation. There were nights when he stayed up playing music, knowing full well Morris needed to be up early. And then, there was the unfortunate night when Morris offered to pay for dinner, and Henry had turned defensive. "I have money," he said, which was only partially true. He worked part-time as a barista, and his parents had stopped sending the monthly check. He didn't even own a credit card.

For years, Morris kept a photograph on display in an old Lennox picture frame he'd inherited from his grandmother. It was taken with a filter to resemble some grainy Polaroid from the 70s. In it, they stood smoking on a balcony with the city lights in the backdrop. Yasmin posed elegantly in her black dress with her creamy shawl covering her shoulders while Morris stood next to her in his oversized shirt reined in by a tight brown vest. His neck was arched as if ready to dive headfirst into her cleavage. Behind them was Henry in his bright pink polo, spinning around towards the camera, flashing a demented smile as some husky man next to him was caught in mid-laugh.

This photo, Morris often told himself, represented the night their little family came together.

They met Yasmin at a party in an Adams Morgan loft that was owned by one of Henry's temporary friends. Yasmin was the only woman in attendance, gliding from conversation to conversation, her facial expressions guarded so no one could read her thoughts; her heavy makeup made her face look masked and brutal. Some of the men fawned over her while others tried to scandalize her, and yet she remained unphased as all of them sought her attention. Even Henry remarked that she had wicked powers and that if he could steal them, he would only use them for evil.

To Morris, she was a refreshing change of scenery. Yasmin was immune to the usual lures of gossip and humble brags; she was the type of person who preferred discussion over simple stories. Together, they sat on the loveseat in the corner, talking about their families and inherited guilt, but also their shared love of British television and nights out at The Black Cat, even though they both agreed the scene was getting tired. Eventually, their wine was drunk, and their conversation stalled, and Morris leaned in with hopes she was amenable.

"Do you like boys or girls?" Yasmin bluntly asked him, and Morris flinched. "I get mixed *vibes* from you."

He drunkenly stared at her and grinned. "It all tastes the same if you close your eyes," he said and immediately regretted it.

She gave him a sour look.

"I'm quoting *Rent*," he stuttered.

"I know," she replied.

He spent the next hour following her about, trying to conjure some newfound wittiness to rewin her approval. Eventually, she relented. He was her only option in a room full of outlandish homosexuals.

It took him a week to finally email her, but when he did, he was surprised at how quickly she responded. Yasmin's tone in words matched her tone in person: short, brisk, and to the point. She'd rather chat in person, she wrote. She was meeting friends at the Brickskellar that evening and encouraged him to join them.

Back then, Morris rarely drank beer and found the menu overwhelming. Hundreds of options were categorized by country of origin in neat little columns. He chose a Sapporo because he liked the name and suffered each bitter sip. Yasmin's friends were two older couples, childless, metropolitan, and heavy drinkers. They went on endlessly about politics, harping on the Bush regime and the endless Iraq War, talking in loud, boisterous voices that dared anyone to challenge them. He felt out of place from the start, and by the end of the evening, a newfound piety beamed in him: this was adulthood, and it was awful.

He went home with Yasmin that night, following her in awkward steps to her efficiency apartment. It was such a tiny space, yet elegantly decorated with overlapping rugs and art print collages. He marveled over the neatly organized room for a few moments before she guided him towards the platform bed and discarded each perfectly arranged pillow. Their sex did not last long, but it was satisfying enough that they lay together for another hour or two, listening to her jazz albums. Occasionally, Yasmin would light a cigarette and delicately ash it into the brass peacock dish on her nightstand.

"My friends will be discussing this," she finally said. "They're not used to seeing me as the older woman."

He forced a smile as Yasmin's body turned so she could face him, gently draping a muscular leg over his, her large foot curved around as if to snare him.

"You were very quiet tonight," she added.

"I wanted your friends to like me," he said nervously.

"They don't know you well enough to like you."

"Well, they seem very smart. You're very smart. I didn't want to embarrass myself."

"They're also very boring at times. You're not boring. That's why you got your invitation." Yasmin's dark eyes brightened. She nestled deeper into her pillow, her dark hair covering her naked shoulders like a shroud. "Tell me a story, a funny one."

"I can't think of anything right now," he said. All that came to mind was the drama of the newspaper staff, though none of it was particularly funny. "I'm not very sophisticated. You'd be bored."

"That's ok," she relented. "It's alright to be bored sometimes."

*

Yasmin's first love affair was with the film Dangerous Liaisons. She was fourteen, a painfully serious girl, who had been drawn in by the elaborate costumes and set designs, but entirely enamored with the social politics of the French aristocracy. She watched the film with near-religious devotion and developed a fantasy in which she was Uma Thurman's Cecile de Volanges, dressed in her ornate gowns, taking instructions from Glenn Close's Marquise Isabelle de Merteuil. Only in Yasmin's version, Cecile was an apt pupil who thwarted Valmont and inherited his estate.

Not only was the film central to her sexual awakening, but it was also the bridge to her adult self. Inspired by Merteuil, she practiced detachment; she listened and observed; she learned how to always appear cheerful while, under the table, she stuck a fork into her hand.

By the time she entered college, she had perfected poised stoicism, was always congenial, and could walk that balance beam between wit and vulgarity. She had developed a raspy intelligent edge to her voice, something that seemed part femme fatale and part *Sunset Boulevard*, as if, honey, she'd been there and back again and sometimes knew you just needed a cup of tea and a chat to sort things out—a strange affectation in a college freshman but one that made her compelling to others.

For her twenty-first birthday, she avoided the tired old traps of her classmates, drinking their way up and down the Adams Morgan strip, but instead celebrated with the staff of her summer internship at an auction house. They took her to a local wine bar, where she drank very little and asked more questions than answered. By the end of the evening, she was alone with two flamboyantly drunk men, listening as they reminisced about their New York City days in leather bars where men pissed on other men.

"Oh, your virgin ears," they kept saying. "We're disgusting you, aren't we?"

"No." She lit her cigarette. "I'm waiting for you to recommend where I should go next."

A week later, she hunted down one of them in his office. "I'm reading Faggots by Larry Kramer, and I have questions. What are you doing for lunch?" The following summer, he served as a reference for her first job at the Phillip's Collection, and she had continued to move through such circles ever since.

Her affair with Morris was meant to be short-lived, maybe a few weeks at most, as young men often start as fiercely loving kittens but quickly grow into arrogant, self-indulgent cats. They strayed and sometimes never came back; she thought it was inevitable. And besides, Morris was young, both in age and mind, a silly little man who had no direction, who liked to play games and read fantasy, and who did not yet care about his place in the world. This also made him appealing. Morris was unpretentious. He was kind to strangers and repulsive people. He sometimes mentioned the conspiracy theorist who came into the newspaper offices every few months, a distressed man who wore army fatigues and would drop handwritten manifestos on their desks. The rest of the staff would hide from him, but apparently, Morris would sit with him for an hour each time, patiently listening until the man wore himself out. *Who does that?*

*

Morris liked the idea of compiling the different fragments of his life and welding them together into something compact and easily maintained. He found the perfect apartment in Arlington that was big enough for the three of them. For Henry, it was closer to the city and better for his job search. The rent was ideal for Yasmin, who was starting her MBA in the Fall. They all knew it was a bad idea, but they did it anyway.

They moved in over Memorial Day weekend, with one last intoxicating summer ahead of them. Every Friday evening, they assembled and drove into the city, abandoning their car wherever was convenient and visiting the same sushi restaurant where the servers knew their orders by heart. They would feast on sashimi pieces and drink hot sake from thimble-shaped cups. Then, they would walk to the edge of Dupont Circle for their evening espressos until some acquaintance would surely drag them out to a bar or house party. Whatever happened, they rarely came home before dawn. Saturday evenings were reserved for the clubs, where they danced and dispersed and somehow always found each other and returned to their lair at the café for morning bagels. Then, they returned home to sleep. By Sunday night, they were haggard and sore, watching movies on the couch, their limbs intertwined until the last cigarettes were smoked, and they would retire to their separate rooms. The rest of the week, they lived normal lives until Friday came again, and it was time to go out.

Sometimes, Morris slept in Yasmin's room; other nights, he didn't. She had other lovers and encouraged him to do the same. It was practical. They were too young to be committed to just one person and would regret it later if they did. And he agreed. He liked their arrangement and enjoyed bragging about it to his other friends, even if he secretly felt ambivalent.

Morris began to see the summer as a long buffet where they feasted on prime-cut steaks and crisp potato wedges, bowls of olives and cheese, custards, and gooey pies and drank from wine goblets that refilled themselves. Each bite was its own pleasure, but it came with the hovering dread that eating too much could cause sickness; not eating enough meant food would spoil, and eventually, someone would need to clean up the mess.

"You're overthinking," Henry told him. "Stop worrying and enjoy yourself. Nothing lasts forever."

"That's exactly what I'm worried about."

The summer ended, and the threads that bound them all snapped asynchronously. Yasmin started grad school and moved through her cycle of work, school, and projects, her linen skirts swaying as she skittered past them, almost doe-like. Morris, too, felt the sudden pressures of productivity. Someone in the loose hierarchy of the newspaper decided he could be doing more. His comings and goings were suddenly carefully monitored, as he was now responsible for all the bookkeeping and spent his evenings taking design courses at the local community college. In the span of a month, their summer lives dissolved completely.

Nothing changed for Henry. His grand schemes, whatever they were, never came to fruition. He continued working at the coffee shop and picked catering jobs for extra money, which he recklessly burned through. He continued with his old habits: the late-night jaunts into DC, disappearing until dawn, only now with a budding resentment that his regular playmates rarely joined him. On those evenings he was home, he sat around and complained, anxious to know what they thought of so-and-so not calling him back or explaining how some unforeseen circumstance had ruined what should have been a perfect night out. There were evenings of canceled plans and no money when he would pace around the apartment, scowling and searching for an argument. Sometimes, Morris would come home from work and find Henry draped over the couch like a discarded rag doll, spilling his tea as Yasmin patiently listened.

There were occasional nights when Henry bullied him out, and Morris felt tethered and yanked from restaurant to café until he was sitting at the bar of Apex, feeling the weight of cigarettes and booze in his gut.

"Alright, here's what's happening," Henry said. "That guy there has invited us over—he has coke."

Morris felt the color fade from his skin and turned his head. He felt nauseous; he wanted to go home.

"Dude, you're in the Tunnel. Snap out of it."

"Stop saying that," Morris snapped. "I don't even know what it means anymore."

*

They dispersed for the holidays, their first real break from one another. Morris took off the entire week of Christmas to visit his family in Pennsylvania. At first, he dreaded it—he came from an overbearing Irish-Catholic family that valued togetherness over privacy. Yet, on the morning of his train, he felt an intense longing for them, and if not them, for his childhood home. He wanted to rest.

From the moment he arrived, he was whisked into the family bosom and completely absorbed into their steady stream of arranged luncheons and dinners and the parade of relatives, all overeager to make their presence known. Each of these meetings was heavily peppered with questions about his job, his questionable fashion choices, and his plans for the future. He seemed to flicker in and out of conversations, mildly stuttering one moment and coyly smiling the next until they continued without him.

"He's so skinny," his mother exclaimed in front of the aunts. They had thrust mounds of sandwiches in front of him, more than he could ever eat.

"What has he got to wear for pictures?" someone asked.

His mother scowled. "We'll have to fix that," she said. "He can keep the goatee. Not a fan of it, but what's with the chunky glasses?"

"We'll get him a beret," someone said. "Then you can tell everyone we have a poet in the family!" The women laughed in unison as Morris sighed.

Later, his father and brothers rescued him for an afternoon at the bowling alley, where they drank pitchers of beer and cursed over every gutter ball. They were not the type to ask questions but instead made statements and expected others to fill in the gaps. Morris dropped Yasmin's name once or twice, full of flattery, and his father gave him a confused look.

"But Henry still lives there, right? Tell us about him again."

In the evening, he retired to his bedroom, full of his childhood treasures and action figures. The room held echoes of long past masturbation sessions set to Weezer albums, the cryptic music of old Nintendo games, and long stretches of teenage angst, writing in journals and hating everyone. When he closed his eyes, he half-wondered if he would wake up in his teenage body and relive it all over again.

He called Yasmin.

"Is it very horrid there?" she asked playfully.

"Oh yes. Very horrid."

"Good. Maybe next year, I'll join you."

"I think everyone would be pleasantly surprised."

They arrived home to find Henry wallowing on the couch, the air thick with stale cigarette smoke, and the curtains were drawn, which cast the main room in dramatic shadows. He looked miserable, with swollen eyes, puffy cheeks, the youthful hobbit features having melted into a stressed goblin, lying in his own filth.

"I'm never going home again," he said. "I hate them. I hate them all."

It was impossible to know what happened, as Henry gave so many versions. He was always mixing tales and adding in whatever ingredients he felt gave them more flavor. It was clear that his parents had finally cut him off, that there had been a public scene from which none of them could recover. The details changed with every retelling until even Henry was uncertain of what transpired. His parents had tried locking in his room. They had wanted him to see a psychiatrist. There was talk of putting him in a hospital.

"Well, it obviously didn't happen," he said. "I saw the signs and left before it could."

For weeks, Henry didn't go out. After each shift, he returned and laid out his tip money until there was enough to cover his share of the rent. Otherwise, he sat in front of the television or tinkered with his computer. Sometimes, late at night, Morris could hear him pacing around the apartment, talking to himself as if he were addressing a courtroom, laying out the facts as he knew them and why he was not guilty. Other times, he spelled out lists: two packs of light bulbs, a thirty-six-case of toilet paper, two bottles of olive oil, a dozen onions, hand soap… as if he were mentally stockpiling for the apocalypse.

Morris never mentioned any of this. They would sit together on the balcony and talk about their fantasy stories, to which Henry barely contributed. He once asked Henry if he'd been looking for a new job, and Henry sighed. "Can we just talk about fun things right now?"

As the winter receded, so did Henry's darkness. For a while, he was cheerful again. He started venturing back out, luring them to the coffee houses and for the occasional midnight showing at the E Street Cinema. Other times, he went out alone and disappeared for two days, returning with wild stories of his new friends and their fabulous parties.

Then, the café called, looking for him. He'd missed a shift. And after another, they called again to say Henry was no longer employed there. When he finally returned, he looked shallow and drained, the color gone from him.

"Oh well," he said as he buttered his bread. "It was a shitty job, anyway."

One day a cockatiel in a dismal brown cage appeared next to the kitchen door. Henry had rescued it, he said. A friend of his was moving, and the poor creature had no place else to go. The cockatiel was gray, with a velvety yellow throat and large orange circles on its cheek like rouge. Yasmin was clearly disgusted by it but said nothing. Morris didn't mind, except the bird would squawk angrily at him if he got too close. He tried to befriend it, offering it a sunflower seed, and it bit him on the knuckle. Henry giggled.

"He's doing it for attention," Yasmin said drolly and left the room.

Henry often paced around the apartment with the bird perched on his shoulder. Sometimes he would cuddle it and make cooing noises. One night, Yasmin sautéed up a pile of shrimp for scampi and the whole house smelled of acrid seafood.

"We don't like shrimp, do we?" Henry said to the cockatiel.

We? Morris thought.

They wouldn't discuss Henry in the apartment. They knew better. The walls were thin, and they were already aware of every sneeze and fart that took place between the three of them. Instead, Yasmin and Morris took Sunday brunches, sipping from champagne flutes and discussing Henry's awkward behavior. He never seemed to sleep at night and spent the day walking about in with the rigid movements of a zombie. He never seemed to work, yet he always had a little bit of money.

The invasive bird had been there a week when Morris crossed the precipice of Henry's bedroom, intent on having a serious talk. But he was startled by the bare emptiness of the room. The loud movie posters and knick-knacks were all gone, the room surprisingly clean and devoid of personality. He had come in for a confrontation about the cockatiel and the disappearing acts, and the fact rent was due when Henry still owed for the previous month. Instead, he fell into a sentimental speech about the upcoming summer, how he wanted things to go back to the way they were, back to their old habits and how he missed his old friend.

Henry said nothing, and when he crawled into Morris's arms, they felt the Tunnel open up wide, and they were lost deep inside. Suddenly, Morris was kissing Henry hard on the mouth, and the two were naked and bundled in bed, their sex clumsy and mechanical but tender. They awoke hours later to Yasmin standing over them. "Glad you two worked things out," she said. "Now, are we cooking or ordering out?"

The next day, the cockatiel and its cage were gone, leaving only a few seed husks and the lingering smell of bird shit as proof it had ever existed. Henry was sipping wine on the balcony, smiling to himself. "Oh, it was time for him to go back home. All is well."

Morris and Yasmin gave each other skeptical looks.

Everything went back to normal, at least for a little while. Yasmin remained preoccupied with her studies, and Henry continued in his slow breakdown. At night, Morris would lie in bed, listening to the muffled sounds of Henry talking to himself in the next room. He wondered if any of this was ever normal. Was it normal to sleep alone in an apartment shared with two ill-defined lovers, feeling each day like the ticking of a countdown clock?

And then, it ended. Henry walked out one evening with a duffel back slung over his shoulder. "I'm staying with a friend for a few days."

"The rent," Yasmin said almost absently.

"I'm working on it." Henry's voice was pleasant, and his eyes again had that sparkle, their mischievous little gleam, as he twiddled his fingers as he stepped out the door.

They both knew. With what felt like an intuition for the miserable, Morris knew that Henry had never been happy except at the beginning and end of all things.

A few days later, Morris arrived home from work, and the apartment possessed a supernatural feel, hollow and uneven as if its dimensions had changed. On the table sat an overstuffed envelope full of crumpled bills and

Henry's keys. His room was striped clean, the furniture naked, his mounds of CDs and books all gone, as if his entire presence had been struck from the record.

When Yasmin got home, she made tea and poured them into little floral cups she saved for special occasions. She took her time, slicing out lemon wedges and arranging them on the serving dish with the sugar bowl. She loaded everything onto a tray and took it to the balcony. The glass ashtray was gone, so she held her cigarette over the rail to ash.

"Where do you think he went?" Morris asked.

"Probably wherever that fucking bird went." She turned soft and gently rubbed Morris's hand. "How are you doing?"

"I think I'm in shock. People don't just leave like this, or at least they shouldn't."

"He wasn't happy here. And it's not your fault. You're not responsible for someone else's happiness."

"But are we going to be happy now?"

When someone disappears, they still leave fragments of themselves behind. Henry was in their photos and old email chains. There were little tokens of him left to discover: a comb, a lighter, a glass bowl, a mug. He became a lingering phantom in their favorite restaurants. Sometimes, late at night, there was a shuffling noise, the sound of footsteps in the third bedroom, but when they went to investigate, it was always empty. Sometimes, he'd take the Metro into the city and spend an evening in the old café, always sitting in the corner where he had the best view of the door. He'd drink his coffee ceremoniously, as if he were drinking Henry down, letting him settle in his stomach. And should a common acquaintance enter, he always left to avoid conversation.

He called Henry once. It went straight to voicemail. "Hey, it's me. Wanted to check in and see how you're holding up. Call me back." A week later, he called again, but the line was disconnected.

Life moved on. They still had jobs and projects and other friends to keep them company. They downgraded to a two-bedroom apartment. Morris got a raise and quit smoking, and Yasmin completed her MBA. They started going out again, along the Adams Morgan strip and up through the U Street Corridor. On nights when they didn't feel like being social, they bundled together with pillows on the couch, reading books and discussing their other lovers, who were slowly being converted into simple friends. Eventually, they gave up on keeping two separate bedrooms, combining into one and turning the other into an office. Over time, everything felt normal. He was comfortable now, able to ignore that the world was a little less bright and more predictable. It wasn't that the wine had lost its flavor. After a few sips, he was satisfied; there was never any reason to finish the bottle.

And then, there were the quiet moments, those nights out on the balcony, when there wasn't anything to do, and Morris would be left alone with his thoughts. He'd sit there trying to conjure old feelings, longing for those late nights out with the sickening excitement of dark rooms and stranger's apartments. The streets outside were always clogged with people, and there was the lure of stepping out into the night to join them. Every now and then, he'd peer forward and think he'd see a glimpse of Henry wandering carelessly among the pedestrians below. And then, the image would disappear among the crowd as Morris wondered if it was really him, if he had really seen a fragment of his past.

Come back.

Chapter 3

Morris dreamt of the town and its medieval walkways, the sharp-edged streets that swooped, and the little painted houses that cut into the mountainside. He could smell the fragrant hippie shops selling incense sticks, little cakes, woodcarvings, and beaded jewelry. Then, he stood in the Public House under the shadow of the beer-slinging bartendress as Henry beckoned. The lights went out, and the crowds and the darkness trapped him. He was not sure, but he was convinced some aberration, something monstrous, was hunting him. Frantically, he pushed his way to the front door only to find the staircase gone with an endless drop to the street below. And then, large hands grabbed him, thick as bear claws, pulling him back inside and—*Oh God!*

He was awake, sweating, and sprawled out over his bed. A few moments later, the little gears in his head turned, and he became aware of his surroundings, of the Manderlay Colony, his messy war-torn studio, and worst of all, he became aware of the damp stickiness in his underwear. At first, he was mortified. He, Morris

Hines, age thirty-six, had a wet dream. But then, he began to laugh: how funny that he'd been here a full week and hadn't even accomplished a memorable orgasm.

The power was back; the ceiling fan twirled lazily above while the digital clock blinked in accusatory zeroes. Strands of light crept in through the window shades as the scent of late morning creaked in and hovered like a fog. He moved through a headrush and retrieved his cell phone: it was nearly half past nine. That was when the panic hit him.

His flight departed at noon, and it was at least an hour's drive to the airport. Immediately, his mind scrolled through the list of tasks ahead: he hadn't packed and still had the clean the studio, and his rental car needed to be returned. The list went on.

He hated the act of travel. He hated the timeliness of it, the manic rushing followed by endless waiting, the lack of personal space, and the nagging voice in his head that constantly suggested he forgot something. Years ago, he had unwittingly sabotaged a trip with Yasmin to visit her uncle in Germany. At first, he was thrilled with the idea of it. Butterflies danced in his stomach as he imagined castle tours and eating bratwurst while lederhosen-clad gents sang bar songs in the background. He had genuinely wanted to meet her uncle. But as the trip approached, his anxiety spiked. After all, two weeks was a long time to be away from the newspaper and an even longer time to be in a country where you didn't speak the language. What if he did not like the taste of bratwurst? What else was there to eat in Germany? Soon, he found himself avoiding all mention of the trip as if he could will it out of existence. It wasn't that he let his passport expire on purpose. He had ignored it, hoping the issue would sort itself out on its own until it was too late to get it renewed. Yasmin went alone, leaving him stewing in a broth of relief and envy.

Why he thought about this now was unclear, but the memories hovered over him as he manically rushed around the studio. He grabbed his clothes by the handful and crammed them into his duffel bag, gathered up the loose trash and beer cans, sped washed the dishes, all while thinking about the heaviness of Yasmin's scowl. *Let there be enough time.* He offered a little prayer. *Please don't let me miss my flight.* He showered and dressed and shoved his archaic laptop in his backpack. He had to turn in his dirty linens and the key to the main office at the barn. It was ten o'clock, two hours till his flight; he tried not to think about it.

As he came tumbling out the door, his dirty sheets stuffed in his arms, Mrs. Oglesthorpe was already perched in her nesting place, glaring at him.

"There's a laundry bag for that!" she called out.

He cursed under his breath and returned inside to fetch it.

Her smile was sadistic. "Don't think you're leaving without sweeping up!"

"No time," he called back as he lugged his duffel bag into the car.

"When does your flight leave?"

"Noon!"

"You'll never make it." She lumbered back inside her cabin.

The manic race continued: soon, his car was packed, cabin locked, and keys and linen returned. Around him, mosquitoes hovered in violent swarms; the sun was unusually heavy for October. Already, the pits of his shirt were damp. It was this moment when everything paused, and he did not feel that pressure of time. In the driver's seat, his fingers hovering over the ignition, he stared over the colony, its rows of pastel cottages, and the picturesque barn surrounded by uninterrupted nature. His mind trailed along the walkways toward town and its little dens of mirth. And then, there was the unresolved issue of Henry. He was not ready to leave, and it pained him to do so. His entire life, he was always leaving the party before its climax, and wouldn't it be lovely to see it to the end for a change? One last look, one last sigh, and then the car started, and he was off.

The drive took more than an hour, as if the entire world conspired against him. His GPS conjured roads that didn't exist—he ended up briefly on a small dirt path surrounded by dilapidated houses and corn fields. And then, the old Buick in front of him fell into a narcoleptic trance at every traffic light. As he reentered the local township, traffic grew into a slow drawl that sent him into mild fits. When he finally arrived at the airport, he was delayed further at the rental car depot. The old sweaty attendant had a slow method of running his hands over every inch of the car, searching for dents, and only after his inspection was complete, he muttered, "You don't have to wait here with me. You're good to go."

As Morris rushed into the terminal, he felt a rumbling in his gut, a nasty gurgle that had slowly built through the entire drive. His body rebelled against him, his stomach wheezing as he hovered over the self-check-in port. Another indignity was that his credit card wouldn't register, which sent him to the ticket counter. It was eleven-thirty, and his stomach ached with a new wave of tremors.

"Good morning!" The attendant was a middle-aged woman with bright orange makeup smeared over her face. She seemed oblivious to his discomfort.

Morris gave a trembling watery smile as he pulled his ticket up on his phone. "My plane is taking off soon. Is it too late to check luggage?" He passed his phone to her and prayed she would be quick.

She scanned it, adjusted her glasses, and inspected her screen. "Oh, dear." Her head shook with sympathy. "I'm so sorry, but you just missed it."

Morris stared at her in disbelief. She had spoken the words, and he had heard them, but they made no sense.

"Sir?"

"Oh God, no." The pain in his stomach intensified. "It leaves at noon. Boarding isn't until eleven thirty.

"Oh, bless your heart. Takeoff was eleven thirty, dear."

Morris winced, and panic flushed over him. He didn't have the energy to argue. "What about another flight? I need to make my connection in Charlotte."

Nimble fingers danced along the keyboard. "We can do Monday morning," she said. "What about Chicago? It's not quite the right direction, though, and you'd have to wait on standby."

"No other flights today?" He felt the people behind him getting agitated.

"Oh, hon. It's Columbus Day weekend. Everybody's traveling."

"But it's Saturday," he said weakly. He felt the urge to argue that Columbus Day shouldn't be celebrated and that there had to be a seat somewhere, but his jaw locked tight.

"I know, I know, but everybody's traveling."

His gut felt like someone had blown an air bubble into him, and it was close to popping. As Morris leaned forward, the sweats started.

"Are you okay?" the woman said. "You don't look right."

Of course, he wasn't. He was going to be sick, all indications pointed to being violently sick. The man behind him cleared his throat. Did they not understand he was in distress?

"I need the restroom," he stammered as the attendant nodded sympathetically.

The lavatory was a marvel of ugly aqua-colored tiles, a landlocked state's vision of the sea. He dashed into the farthest stall, propped his bags against the door, and emptied his bowels, cringing and straining throughout a long, painful process that left him feeling depleted. In the end, he was gasping in the sickly smells, thankful he was at least spared the indignity of doing this on a plane.

But as he sat there, there was the sad realization that his plane had taken off, and much like that fabled trip to Germany, he was left behind. Yasmin would be furious.

And if not furious, disappointed, which was worse because it would shadow him for weeks. He imagined her at their dining table, anticipating his return, a cup of tea nearby as she delicately licked a finger to turn the page of her book. He could clearly see her two faces juxtaposed against each other. The first, her kind eyes and soft smile, an aerie expression as comforting as ice cream; the other, her stern, hard-lined face, jaw clenched as if slowly chewing down her dissatisfaction. Lately, he'd seen the second version more and more, and now, he knew he'd see it again.

When his stomach finally settled, he returned to the counter. The previous woman was gone and replaced with a portly young man wearing huge oval glasses. "Can I help you?" the attendant demanded.

"Oh, there was a lady here a few minutes ago. Is she coming back?"

"Who?" The man gave him a defensive glare as if the question offended him.

"Never mind." Once again, Morris moved away and idled by the newspaper stand, contemplating a coffee. From across the terminal, the attendant glared at him with deep concentration. Perhaps he fit the description of one of those fabled suspicious persons travelers were warned about.

Moments later, he was outside, pacing along the kiss and ride. He called Yasmin.

"Shouldn't you have left already?" she asked.

"Hi, sweetie," he said and winced as she chirped on the other end. They weren't the type for pet names.

"Well, sweetie," she responded, "is this the part when you tell me your flight's delayed?" There was distilled noise of street life in the background—she was out on the balcony, probably smoking.

"We'll get to that. But first, you won't believe who I ran into last night..."

There was a little pause on the other end when he evoked Henry's name. "Seriously? Are you sure?"

"Oh yes. We talked. Kind of."

"That's insane." He could feel her pacing now. "I have so many questions. Lots of them... Are you alright?"

"He looked awful."

"What? Has he gotten fat? You know that happens to people when they get older. Especially skinny guys who sit around all day playing video games. Keep that in mind."

"Don't be like that. And yes—he's heavier, but that's not it. He looked bad, really bad, like damaged." The first image that came to mind was the burn marks. He described Henry in detail, from his tired drooping eyes to his squishy belly, but his hand... Morris couldn't bring himself to speak of it.

"Unfortunately, none of this surprises me," Yasmin said. "So, what's his story? Does he live there? Is he a homeless drug addict now?"

"I don't know. He lives here, I guess, but he didn't go into details. The whole situation was weird. I was in a bar, and next thing I know, he's tapping me on the shoulder and talking shit, and then, the moment I met his friends, he was trying to get rid of me."

Yasmin sighed. "Sounds like him. There wasn't a scene, was there?"

"No scene, no argument, nothing. And then there was a blackout, the whole town went dark, and I left without even saying goodbye. I feel weird about it. He looked miserable."

"I'm sorry to hear it." He heard the sliding door open as she moved back inside. "Are you sure you're okay?"

There were hushed voices in the background. "Do you have a guest?" he asked.

"Yeah. Jenny and Grant. Leo's here too. He's been telling us all about his new boyfriend. Sounds to me like a catty little bitch." Somewhere in the apartment, a shrill voice yelled, "I heard that!" followed by laughter. "We've been drinking mimosas. It rained all week, but today is finally lovely. Everyone's talking about catching a movie later, but I'm not sure I should go. What time does your plane land?" He felt himself mentally fumble. Yasmin knew what time he was supposed to land. She arranged it. She kept notes. She wanted to hear him say it. "Morris? Are you still there?"

"Looks like I'll be back on Monday."

"Understood," she said dismally. "I guess the reunion was that good."

"Don't be mean. It wasn't very pleasant. And I'm an idiot. The power was out, so my alarm didn't go off, and I overslept this morning. The next available flight home is Monday. I wasn't planning on this."

"Neither was I," she said. Her attention was drifting away from him. "Do you have this handled?"

"Yeh, I'm taking care of it. I gotta let the office know as well."

"Monday's a holiday," Yasmin said.

"You know the paper doesn't close."

"Right. In any case, I need to get back to my guests. We should have a long talk about all this when you're home." Her voice was vacant and unsentimental. She could have been talking to anyone. "If you run into Henry again, give him my regards but not my contact info, and don't give him our address. I don't want to reopen that door." He promised—a promise he wasn't sure he could keep. "Goodbye, Morris. See you Monday."

He said goodbye as the call dropped into dead space. He stood there quietly for several moments, staring into the distance, trying to decide what to do next. He needed to buy a new ticket home, but then what? There was nothing close to the airport. A nearby orchard of trees slowly changed into Autumn's bold reds and golds. A mile down the road were the hotels, chain restaurants, and morose strip malls all clumped together. He sighed deeply as he imagined wasting two days away in a hotel room or getting drunk at the local Applebee's. He sighed deeply. There was no point in staying around here.

He left the airport with a fresh plane ticket as the giddiness bubbled up within him. "Where to, friend?" the cab driver asked, and Morris smiled. Where to, indeed. And then, they drove along the highway, and along the country roads, and up through the hills until he stepped out into the familiar little town where the streets were alive. Women with honey-colored shoulders and their freckled children ogled store windows while men sat in clusters on little patios, playing backgammon and smoking cheap cigarillos. A street performer fiddled for loose change tossed in his open case.

He slipped into a terrarium-like bar with extended windows displaying oversized plants. Inside, it was smoky and bright, and he took a seat in the back corner to not disrupt the performing folk singer. A waitress brought him a beer and a fried chicken sandwich with mounds of greasy fries. It was approaching late afternoon, and the bar was filled with a mismatched collective of bikers, hipsters, and Midwestern families, all talking, drinking, and clapping after each song.

Morris allowed himself a pack of Marlboros for the first time in years, lighting up the first one and holding the smoke in his lungs as if it were a joint. He had forgotten the simple pleasure of a cigarette, a way to occupy one's hands, the image it created: that a lone smoker looks like they're waiting for something or contemplating some abstract idea. A smoker had stories to tell; they had secrets. Artists were the best smokers.

For the rest of the afternoon, he sat there until the pack was half empty and his cell phone's battery was near dead. He made small talk with two men, brothers, who were traveling across the country in a camper. They were a jolly pair, egg-shaped and sunburnt and basking in the glory of retirement. They had stories about places and not people, and it was a polite affair. When they left, Morris was relieved but also anxious for someone new to approach him.

Afterward, he walked to Basin Park and sat for a while. A woman was selling trinkets on a large blanket: silver bracelets, wired rings, and little beaded earrings she had made from scratch. He marveled at how they were all so neatly organized.

The streetlamps let out their soft glow as it grew dark, and people dressed up and filled the restaurants. It occurred to Morris that he still needed to secure a place to stay. There were hotels everywhere, from motels and little guesthouses to the grandiose Stoney Brook Manor that loomed over the park, a full buffet of options that he found empty. Above the entrance of the Stoney Brook was the blaring red sign: NO VACANCY. He moved on to another hotel to find the same. Even the scattered B&Bs were revealed to be full. The final weekend of the season, he kept hearing. Nothing was available. Then, his discomfort began to rise.

I'm an idiot. I shouldn't have come back.

Sure, there were other places on the outskirts of town, those no-frill motor lodges that sat sentinel on the roads leading out towards the highway. But it was such a long walk, especially when carting around luggage. At some point, he'd need to take a cab back to the airport, where options were abundant. Except, there were no cabs. Aside from the one that brought him, he had not seen a single yellow taxi car idling for customers. For a moment, there was the lure of the bars. At least he could squat for a while, charge up his phone, and maybe flirt his way into someone's hotel room. Then came the ridiculous notion that Henry would arrive, tickled to find his former friend in such a predicament. Henry would be obligated to help him, he was certain. But then, what were the chances of Henry finding him two nights in a row?

The only other option that came to mind was the Manderlay Colony. It would be dinner time soon, and the residents would all gather together in the barn. He'd not been gone long enough to be forgotten. Even Mrs. Oglesthorpe wouldn't be so cold-hearted to leave him sleeping on the streets.

He pulled up Manderlay on his phone and dialed the number. Even if it was Saturday night and the director had gone home for the weekend, there were still the cooks and the office attendant. And suddenly, the phone rang as he stood there, feeling foolish and ill-prepared.

"Good evening," a voice came from the other end, one Morris did not recognize. It was a young woman, maybe even a teenager, a disembodied innocent voice that practically giggled. "How can I help you?" she half-sung.

"Yes, this is Morris Hines. I've stayed at Manderlay this past week," he began.

"Oh, Mr. Hines! What can I do for you?"

He tried to place her voice, but he couldn't parse it. Perhaps she was one of the cooks or the intern he'd seen loitering around the main office. It didn't matter. He spat out a small rendition of his situation, careful not to go into full details. "You see, I'm in a bind. I'm now here till Monday, but I don't have any place to stay."

"Oh no! And you can't get a hotel?"

"Well, if I could, I wouldn't be calling." He winced. That came out rude, and he was in no position to be anything less than gracious. The voice giggled, a girlish youthful sound, the kind usually accompanied by twiddling fingers. "I was wondering if I could extend my stay by another night or two. I'd greatly appreciate it."

"Give me a moment, please," and the line went silent for several agonizing minutes. "Looks like you were in Cabin 3, yes? No one is moving in until tomorrow afternoon. You can use it tonight, but there won't be any bedsheets."

"That would be perfect. Thank you so much!"

"No problem. I'll go unlock the door for you before I head out." Her voice was buttery and sweet, the kind of voice you spread like jam. "But this is against the rules," she added. "And some of the other residents might not approve. I recommend getting here as quickly as you can. They'll be at dinner soon, so now's a good time to head up. Please be discreet and head out before breakfast, ok?"

"Of course, of course." He thanked her profusely. "Oh, and who am I speaking with?" he asked, but she had already hung up.

By the time he reached the colony, the evening had shrouded the town in purple shadows with the lampposts guiding his way. He crossed the small bridge and through the carport until the cottages were in view, all dark except for the stray porch light. In the distance, the barn was illuminated; thankfully, the other residents were still at dinner. He sprinted across the property until he reached his door but found it locked against him. How odd. He tried the knob again and pushed hard, but the door held steady. He was befuddled—the girl had told him it would be unlocked. He moved to the windows and peered inside. With the curtains drawn, he couldn't tell if it was occupied.

Be discreet. Those were his instructions. He crossed around the back of the cabin, stepping over the rows of ferns, and peered in through the back windows. Even in the low light, he could see the naked mattress and the open doors of the empty wardrobe. He placed his hands cautiously against the window and pushed upward. It moved! He hadn't locked the window that morning. He crawled inside and rushed to the front door, where his bags awaited him. What luck—there were no witnesses.

For a long time, he squatted in the darkness, playing on his phone until he could hear voices echo through the courtyard. The other residents had emerged from dinner and were now making their way across the property. His heart beat furiously with the thrill of trespass as he half-expected someone to unlock the front door, step inside, and catch him.

But no one came. There was no jiggling of the lock, no creaky steps on the front porch. Outside, the other residents dispersed back to their rooms. In the distance, he heard a car engine rev—perhaps a few of them were going into town. After a few breathless moments, tranquil silence once again reigned over the colony's courtyard. Eventually, he rose quietly and peered out through the curtains. No one was out. Through a side window, he glimpsed Mrs. Oglesthorpe on her porch, short and stout and standing guard. Ever vigilant.

There was a pleasure in spying on her. He felt a childlike mischief rise in him with the delightful urge to tap on the window in hopes of spooking her. But then, Mrs. Oglesthorpe was the bold type who would come marching over in an instant to investigate. Smiling, he moved away from the window with the pleasure of a ghost, drifting through the rooms of the cabin, mind wandering, happily thinking of old games and fantasy books and leisurely childhood summers when he used to stay up as late as he could to see if he could make it to sunrise. When it was late enough, he haunted the bed, the naked mattress cool against his back, and while he wasn't comfortable, he was tired, staring into the hypnotic twirl of the ceiling fan. *This is what people do when they're happy.* He yawned and scratched the tip of his nose. *They lie on their backs and think about how happy they are.*

Throughout the night, he did not dream, or at least his dreams were pleasant enough to be forgettable. It was a heavy sleep, the kind one needed to shake themselves from in the morning. He arose to the sound of birds and the smell of shaved wood and the cool breeze of the ceiling fan, and the streaks of warm light coming in from the windows. Even without his morning rituals, coffee, radio music, and Yasmin's body next to him, he felt the giddiness of a stowaway. How delightful it was to break the rules and get away with it. The thought tickled him. Spying through the windows, he saw the slow progression of the other residents toward the barn for breakfast. Early morning. Plenty of time.

A full day to play. A full day to play.

First, he would find appropriate lodgings in town. No, first, he would need to sneak off the property. But a quick whiff of his underarms told him he should shower first. There was a thin layer of soap left in the washroom, and he took his time bathing, scrubbed himself clean, and shook himself dry. Then he redressed in clothes that seemed the least dirty.

By the time Morris was ready, physically and mentally, he heard activity in the central courtyard. The other colonists were out and about, enjoying their Sunday morning, sipping from coffee cups and nursing hangovers. Outside, Mrs. Oglesthorpe was talking to someone in her lectern voice as Morris eavesdropped. "Something I've noticed as I've gotten older is my sensitivity to nature. I actually feel rejuvenated by it. And it feeds my work," she was saying. "This place is my salvation."

Morris stifled a laugh. What a ridiculous woman.

The conversation outside stretched and expanded. He had stationed himself under the front windows, peering out every few minutes. He saw at least four people loitering in the courtyard and another two sitting on the porch of an adjacent cabin. It seemed the opportunity to leave undetected had passed, and he grew increasingly impatient. Sundays were, biblically speaking, days of rest, and the entire colony was taking advantage of it. If he walked out now, it would be a spectacle. He could imagine the blank stares as he emerged, with Mrs.

Oglesthorpe loudly demanding, "What are you still doing here?" Even if he had permission, it wouldn't stop her from chastising him. Another hour passed, and people still lingered about. He grew bored, then nervous, and retreated to the bedroom, wondering if he should exit the way he came. But then, getting caught sneaking out a window would look even worse.

Suddenly, there was activity from the front of the cabin: the sound of a key penetrating a lock followed by the front door wheezing open. In a panic, Morris closed the bedroom door and peered through the crack. It was one of the groundskeepers, a potbellied man with a fiery head of shaggy red hair, an abrupt fellow he had avoided throughout the previous week. Inside, the man lumbered, holding a laundry bag and a crate of cleaning supplies, and once he seemed confident he was out of range, he let out a booming fart and chuckled as he did so.

There was no escaping now. The groundskeeper was walking forward, arms full of folded bedsheets, and as he kicked open the bedroom door, he let out an undignified shriek as he found Morris standing there with his bags. For a moment, it seemed like a heart attack; the man had dropped the linens and clutched his chest with long labored breaths. Thankfully, the wheezing changed into laughter, a burst of contagious laughter that Morris echoed as best he could. "Mr. Hines! Good God, you scared me!" But once he regained composure, his face hardened as an eyebrow arched upward. "You left yesterday."

Morris stared miserably. "On my way out now."

"That was yesterday. I saw you drive off."

"Well, I called. I got an extension till this morning." Morris struggled to recount the conversation from the previous night. He regretted not getting the girl's name.

"But you *are* leaving now, right?"

Morris winced. His face glowed bright red with embarrassment. "Yes, of course. Right now, in fact." The man let out a chuckle as Morris collected his bags and squeezed passed him. "Sorry again for startling you," he said, making his way to the front door.

"Poor little Morris," the groundskeeper said. "Not ready to go home."

Outside, the impervious Mrs. Oglesthorpe, with the intuition for the wicked, was waiting, arms crossed, her kimono sleeves dropping with the sharp curve of silky knives. It was a pose he assumed had terrified schoolchildren for decades. "Unbelievable," she muttered.

The other residents were outside, hovering in the grassy courtyard, seated on their porches, all observing with amused distaste. A black bucket of embarrassment tipped itself over Morris's head. He was mortified, speed walking his way off the property, knowing he could never go back.

Chapter 4

Across town, people departed in a mass exodus. As he made his way downtown, Morris felt like he was navigating an obstacle course. He weaved in and out of the way of impatient travelers, idle smokers, and people hovering with their luggage. The streets were clogged with a parade of cars, in which ghost-faced children stared out the back windows, waving at no one in particular. The B&Bs had gone silent and dark and were shuttered as if abandoned. Even the trees were patchy with bright oranges and reds, a reminder that the promiscuity of summer had finally ended.

He reached downtown with his duffel bag slung over his shoulder, watching the crowds thin. On the edge of Basin Park, a lone marionette performer dazzled two awe-struck girls as their parents tried to pull them away. He passed the display window of an art gallery with a prominent sign that read CLOSED FOR WINTER in large multicolored letters. In the distance, the clock tower chimed with its mechanical dong. Funny that he hadn't heard the chime before, not once in the previous week, and now it was oppressively loud, nagging the tourists to keep on schedule. Time to go, it said.

Not leaving yet. Sorry, he thought as he entered the hotel.

The foyer of the Stoney Brook Hotel was a gawdy pretense, an advertiser's idea of a haunted Victorian showroom. It was filled with antique furniture, peeling wallpaper, and other ornaments, including a wood-carved swan in mid-flight that was suspended near the staircase. Morris found himself instantly charmed. He plucked a brochure from the nearby display case, which gave a watered-down history of the Stoney Brook. Originally built as a sanitarium, it was closed after several mysterious deaths. The hotel was a certified haunted site and boasted numerous resident spirits. They offered ghost tours most nights, a monthly séance, and a daily continental breakfast. It was perfect.

As the last of the tourists departed, Morris went to the counter and booked a room.

"You'll be one of the few people here," the attendant said. "You'll practically have the hotel to yourself." Unlike the other smiling denizens, Kenneth, as his name tag read, was a stoic young man who spoke in a tone of droll boredom. He gave a deadpan recitation of the brochure with the same enthusiasm as one mentions the weather. "Tours no longer run during the week, so I can put you on the haunted floor if you like. But you need to be out by Friday."

"I only need one night," Morris said. "Whatever's cheapest."

"Eighty a night. Sixth floor. The restaurant's on the second level. The kitchen closes early on Sunday nights. Breakfast in the lounge." Kenneth pointed to the foyer's side room before retrieving two brass keys. "First one is your room; the second one opens the front door. We lock up at nine. If you get locked out, call the number posted out front." Morris handed over his credit card. "Thank you, Mr. Hines," Kenneth said and stared into grim space.

His room was embellished with dark wallpaper, oval framed photographs, and bronze table lamps. The four-post bed held a crotchet doily, long and yellowed with age. Despite the flat-screen television, it all felt plucked from the set of a costume drama. He pulled back the heavy drapes and gazed over the town, the flat rooftop buildings, the pastel awnings, the clogged arteries of streets, and the dwindling tourists in their slow march home; one day left, and he was eager to go out and meet it.

But first, he wrote an email to Yasmin. He missed her terribly, a point he hammered in until it was almost gratuitous. "Nothing exciting has happened yet," he wrote. "I don't think I'm good at being on my own like this. If you were here, things would be different." He described the hotel, the bars, and the little grottos amongst the medieval streets. It felt important to stretch it out as long as possible until he finally typed Henry's name. "I'm equally dreading and hoping to run into him again. If the other night was a test, I think I failed it. Just once, I'd like a do-over," he said. That was enough. No point in dwelling on it. He assured her his flight home was booked and he'd be back Monday afternoon and signed off with Xs and Os. Then, he sent an email to the newspaper editor, a short and sweet one. His flight was canceled, he claimed, and he was temporarily stranded. But he would be back at work Tuesday morning, eager to catch up, and apologized for the inconvenience. He hit the "send" button and smiled as he did it.

Back outside, the breeze picked up. Morris sat on the edge of Basin Park, admiring the central water fountain. He smoked a cigarette. He smoked three cigarettes. He went to a bodega, the Inn-Convenience Store, and bought another pack.

As Morris walked up the hill, a distressed figure came into his line of sight. It was a short man with bushy brown hair, hovering mid-sidewalk with his hand extended, begging from everyone, looking at no one. Despite his haggard appearance, the man was still poised. His torn cardigan and flowing pants were drably color-coordinated; his stance showed the confidence of some monstrous toy dog that didn't realize how ugly it was.

Aghast, Morris ducked around a corner and leaned against the wall, listening to his miserable heartbeat. The man looked exactly like Henry. The loose rags, the vacant stare, and the curly cherub's head recalled Henry. But that was impossible. Two nights ago, they drank together in a bar with no tell-tale signs of homelessness. Henry had been amongst friends, and they didn't seem like the type who'd allow one of their own to beg on the streets. Still, anything was possible.

He felt like a coward hiding there, but what on earth did one do in this situation? He furiously typed into the browser on his iPhone: "how to handle seeing a friend homeless." The phone mused over it before producing a sprawling list of articles, and the first link presented a bullet-point list: "Let them tell their story. Offer small gifts of food and clothing. Pray with them..." Morris put his phone away. This was absurd.

Of course, he knew he couldn't hide forever. He was obligated to help Henry, at least buy him a meal, and then would come the daunting task of getting in touch with his parents. Yet, the longer he crouched there, the more he descended into schadenfreude. There was a part of Morris, that snarky vengeful part, that immensely enjoyed the idea of Henry the Panhandler. And then came the masturbatory fantasy of Henry trying to resist his help, all the bartering, and pleading before he eventually crumbled. *Oh, how the mighty have fallen.*

Morris stepped back out onto the sidewalk, but Henry was gone. No, there he was, across the street, slumped against a building, head bowed as if in prayer. Quickly, Morris ran up to him only to realize it was not Henry. The panhandler looked nothing like him at all. His face was gaunt and leathery, hair not quite curly as it was stringy. He was much older than he appeared from a distance.

Just as the panhandler took notice of him, Morris ducked into a café. The smugness was gone and instantly replaced by a cold spectrum of emotions: a range of horror and guilt that made him shiver. Only a monster would wish such circumstances on a friend, even an ex-friend, and that made him ugly, as ugly as the scars on Henry's hand. As he waded through a stupor, a server pranced forward, cradling a coffee urn to his chest.

"Can I get you a table?"

"*What?*" Morris blundered. The server was a jolly little man who almost bounced in place. Apparently, he saw no monster before him.

"Sir? Are you all right?"

"Yes," Morris replied. "I'm sorry. I'm a little scatterbrained today. Table for one, please."

The young man gave a sweeping gesture over the empty café. Morris chose a table in the back, far away from the picturesque windows, and ordered a sandwich overflowing with chunks of tomatoes and artichoke hearts and a heavy dose of mayonnaise drizzled onto the plate. Eating was a comforting act, an ideal passed down through his family, but the meal was not enough to prevent his mind from wandering back to his encounter with the panhandler, replaying that moment as if it was Henry and what might have happened. This encouraged other questions. If Henry wasn't homeless, what was he doing here? How did he survive? And how would he react if they crossed each other's paths on the street? He imagined a look of surprise, a snide little grin, and then the same ghosting act of passing by without a word.

"Anything else?" The server hovered close throughout the meal as if trying to anticipate some unspoken need.

The poor kid was probably bored.

"Doing fine. Just the check, please."

The server returned quickly; the bill was very inexpensive. "Last day in town?"

"Yup. I leave tomorrow morning."

"Well, I recommend the sculpture garden if you haven't seen it. It's one of my favorite places," the young man said. Even after he paid, the server was still hovering there with an eager smile.

In a town like this, it was easy to fall into the sin of sloth. The town was not large, and there was little to do besides eat and drink. Morris passed a rustic theater house and an Escape Room, both closed, and then a vintage arcade where a few feral teenagers scavenged for quarters. From several vantage points, the colossal Jesus statue was in full view from the neighboring ridge. He had considered hiking up to it, but there were no marked roads or trails, which made it seem not worth the effort. By early afternoon, he descended to the River Walk along Flood Street. The river was more of a tepid stream that gurgled alongside the paved walkways, but Flood Street possessed a near-European charm. Quaint antique shops and café patios sat in orderly rows on either side with no reason to believe they were ever in danger of flooding.

Eventually, he chose a small pub towards the end, all wooden and creaking and smelling of comfort food. The waitress hunched over a pinball machine while two red-capped trucker types cheered.

"Hon, you sit anywhere," she called out. "Baby's on a winning streak!" The pinball machine exploded with flashing lights and beeps.

There weren't many customers left. A well-dressed family clustered in a booth, silently praying over the meal. Another group, perhaps a stag party dressed in matching Hawaiian shirts, toasted and heckled the exasperated groom-to-be. Near them, two plump girls scowled together in quiet confidence as if secretly plotting when and how the stag party would die. Otherwise, it was a mellow atmosphere serenaded by the light sounds of country music coming in through the speakers. This was the last place Henry would come, but then, Henry was a night creature. There was no point in looking for him now.

When the dancing lights of the pinball machine finally stopped, the waitress took his order and deposited a whiskey and ginger on his table. The drink was strong. One sip and he felt the pleasure of it, the liquor swimming in his veins, and his mind relaxed. A few sips in, the novelty wore off, and he grew restless. When his glass was half-empty, his head turned fuzzy, and he was playing on his phone, scrolling through social media. There was the usual sprawl of political rants and memes, but then there were the joyful photos of his friends out together, enjoying Sunday brunches and backyard get-togethers. Yasmin posted a selfie in the Renwick Gallery, posing with Jenny and Grant in front of the Burning Man exhibit. Envy settled in as he lit a smoke.

When I get back, let's throw a party. When was the

last time he hosted a gathering at the apartment? He smirked at the idea of it. *A welcome home party for my big adventure.* He stared bitterly at the empty bar, wishing for something, anything, to happen.

On his feed, he typed, "Stranded in the Midwest and waiting under a rock to die," and attached a photo of his whiskey and lit cigarette artfully displayed together. But then, after careful thought, he deleted it. Instead, he took a picture of the bar's interior, carefully capturing the front windows and the edge of the pinball machine, and used a filter to accentuate the colors. He added a caption: "Coolest little bar near the river. They don't make places like this anymore." After a few minutes, the post garnered a few likes. His friend Michael was the first to respond: "I'll be there in ten minutes," punctuated with a smiling emoji. Yasmin commented next: "Have fun. Be safe." Satisfied, he put his phone away.

When you do nothing, you do it slowly and methodically. The afternoon started to recede. He made his drink last as long as possible until the ice fully melted, and he no longer wanted it. He was considering his next steps when a new figure entered with the bravado of a spaghetti western sheriff. The man was oppressively large, wearing the beige uniform of a small-town cop; his shiny badge arrogantly caught the light. Almost immediately, they locked eyes, and the tall man approached his table.

"What the hell are you doing here?" he said in a loud boom of a voice that made Morris flinch. It took several seconds to recognize him, but the details began to come together: the gruff voice, the mutton chops, the red-red mouth. They had met the other night in the Public House. "Did I startle you?" the tall man asked.

"No. I'm sorry—I was lost in thought."

Without invitation, the tall man sat down, looming, if not towering, over the little bar table. The proportion brought to mind a grown man crouched at his daughter's tea party set.

The waitress turned away from the pinball machine. "Atherton, hon, you off duty?"

"I am now," he replied, not bothering to look away at her.

"Atherton," Morris stupidly repeated.

"That's right. But you didn't answer my question. I thought you'd be long gone after you ran out on your bill the other night."

Morris balked. "No, I paid in cash all night." He drank the watered whiskey down in a long gulp.

Atherton tilted his head back and gave an open-mouthed laugh. "I'm joking."

"I'm sorry for running out the other night. I felt a little overwhelmed, and I get anxious around new people."

"Relax." Atherton pointed to Morris's glass. "You're empty. How about another?"

"I shouldn't. I've spent too much already."

"What's that got to with it? I asked if you want another. Not if you wanted to pay for it." Atherton flicked his heavy wrist, and the waitress abandoned her game and brought them a beer and a whiskey. The tall man winked at her as she left. "So, you still haven't answered my question. What are you still doing here?"

Morris sighed. The story seemed so tedious now that it was hardly worth rehashing. He had missed his plane through no fault of his own, and now he was killing time. The real question was: how to use it?

"A good problem to have," Atherton said as they clinked glasses.

They chatted pleasantly about their lives, in which they said much but revealed little. Atherton was a sheriff in a town with almost no crime, which meant freedom to come and go as he pleased. Morris talked about the endless routine of the newspaper. There was one story he loved to tell: years ago, he'd made a bumbling error in an advertisement for their neediest client, Trisha Nguyen. She was a vicious power Realtor who paid a year's worth of advertising in advance and whose cold demeanor struck fear into the hearts of the entire editorial staff. In one unfortunate ad, he had made a tragic little typo in the description of an open house, which was supposed to read: "Gourmet kitchen. New roof. Really huge deck."

"Yasmin hates that story," he said.

They laughed; they drank.

As he reached for his rocks glass, Morris couldn't recall when it had been refilled. It was whiskey, that sweet elixir that encouraged the act of oversharing; he blushed at the thought of the tall man, the town sheriff, buying his drinks. *Are you trying to get me drunk?*

When Henry's name was finally evoked, it hovered over them. They regarded each other cautiously, pressing their feet against the ice, testing to see if it would crack. When it didn't, they boldly stepped forward and furiously discussed Henry and all his incarnations: Henry the flamboyant, Henry the grifter, Henry the dramatic plaything, Henry the mischievous hobbit plucked straight from a fairy tale. It opened all sorts of doors, none thoroughly examined, but enough to peek inside. They both had a history with Henry. This was clear.

"My wife calls him a lost soul," Atherton said into his glass. "Martha can be sentimental. She thinks all men need a little mothering. On the other hand, I think some people need a good whipping from time to time."

Wife? The word echoed with a strange ring to it, a wedding ring, now visible on Atherton's finger. Once Morris saw it, he could only see it.

"You looked surprised."

Morris stammered. "I guess I made some assumptions."

Atherton nodded. "I'm sure most of them are true."

"Does your wife know?"

"Does Yasmin?"

"Yes."

"Yes."

They smiled conspiratorially; they shared a common vice.

Several minutes later, the waitress was summoned, and Atherton paid her with a stack of folded bills. She practically curtsied. "All right then," he said. "Ready to get out of here?" His voice had the commanding tone of a gunshot, and instinctively Morris tensed up before he shook his head. Atherton let out a cruel little laugh. "It's almost suppertime. Where else you gotta be?"

"On a plane," Morris replied drolly. "I have to be up early."

Chase me. I can't promise anything but chase me a little longer.

"Didn't you say that last time?"

He was swimming in whiskey now, neck deep, unsure of how much he'd swallowed. And if the current picked up, he'd easily be dragged under and drown, except for the helping hand that kept him steady. Atherton assisted him with a series of gentle pushes and nudges, out of the bar and down the River Walk.

"Come on now," Atherton said, grip on his shoulder, fingers gently grinding, steering, until they were in Atherton's car, driving past the brightly painted buildings and the last remains of the tourists. Downtown flashed alongside until they were on the wooded lanes that curved toward the mountain.

A familiar feeling gurgled in his belly. Morris was deep in the Tunnel now. "Where are we going?"

"Dinner with friends."

The road ahead ascended and curved; the trees grew thicker. The town practically vanished and was replaced by endless nature, with the occasional glimpse of a cottage in the distance. He quickly lost track of the turns they made until he felt utterly lost among the woods, that familiar nervous energy bubbling in his gut. He knew this feeling well from his college days when he allowed himself to be spirited away to many dark houses and decrepit apartment buildings with no idea of what dangers to expect. Only now, his imagination was running wild. How many horror movies were set around this premise? Around another bend, there was a glimpse of the Christ statue standing vanguard, peering over them.

"Are you taking me to meet Jesus?" he asked suspiciously.

"No. That place isn't for you."

Instead, the car veered onto a small gravel road that led up to an imposing structure. Two adjacent farmhouses were connected by a long privacy fence that snaked along a car lot, all of which was painted the color of moss as if to camouflage it from the view of the main road.

As Morris took in the surroundings, he felt more sober and gave Atherton a skeptical look. "What is this place?"

"Relax," Atherton said. "Call it a gut instinct, but I think you'll like it here."

And then, he felt that same magnetic pull as he followed Atherton out of the car and across the lot until he was being ushered inside. They stood on a stone patio full of umbrellaed tables and a glimmering swimming pool blended into the well-manicured ridge where flowering plants bloomed in their last hurrah. The whole scene came together: this was not a compound at all. It was a secluded inn with the integrity of a private resort. A set of hiking trails led to a scattering of guest cottages partially obscured by the foliage. The pool was clean and bordered by a jacuzzi tub with metal stands holding rolled-up towels. To their right was the covered pavilion that bordered the main house. It had a small open-air bar full of decorations: a hanging stained-glass mural, brightly colored throw pillows, glass ashtrays, and a trio of Greek-replica statues all standing at attention with their little coin purses snug between their legs. And then, Morris recognized another familiar face: Jack, the large man from the other night, giving him a shy nod before returning his attention to the charcoal grill at his side. The place was enchanting; at least, Morris was enchanted by it.

The proprietor was a stout, balding man with bright tattoo sleeves who radiated with near-ferocious hospitality. He came rushing out of the guesthouse and flung his arms around Atherton, who struggled to pry himself free. The man laughed, a deep belly laugh, almost fiendishly jolly. Then, he turned to Morris.

"Welcome to the Oasis. I'm Cook. Look upon my works, ye mighty, and despair!" He let out another laugh.

Morris grinned uncomfortably, eyes darting around. Did this man quote *Ozymandias*? Did he have any idea of what that meant?

"Oh, dear. He's shy," Cook said, looking back to Atherton. "You're always picking up runaways. Whatever will the wife think?"

"Enough," Atherton grumbled.

But Cook remained undeterred. He was instantly gossiping about the various happenings that involved so-and-so and you-know-who until he and Atherton fell into a deep conversation from which Morris was excluded. Again, he locked eyes with Jack, who seemed like the type who was often excluded as well.

"It's too early for those steaks," Cook called over his shoulder, but it was too late. Jack had already dropped one onto the grill. "Well shit, you might as well do them all now."

Morris took the opportunity to extradite himself. He wandered over to the grill and into the shade of Jack's body. How large he was; how timid. He possessed the stature of a titan working his forge, yet as Morris approached, his hands trembled as he laid the next steak out to sizzle. *Gentle giant*, Morris thought. "Do you mind if I join you?"

Jack gave him an uncertain look and wiped the sweat from his brow in a slow, burdened swipe, but he nodded. All right then. They stood together, quietly baking in the heat of the coals, both waiting for the other to speak.

Morris took another turn. "I can't work a grill to save my life."

"Not that hard," Jack mumbled. "People act like it's science."

It was difficult to tease out anything resembling a conversation. Still, Morris pressed. "Remind me, what do you do?"

"I'm a cook."

"What's your specialty?"

"Oh, I don't know. Flat grill meats, bacon, fried eggs, hash. Regular stuff. Collard greens."

"That's nice. And you're from Tulsa, right?"

"Born and raised."

"What brought you out here?"

The gentle giant took his time sprinkling a healthy

dose of lemon pepper across the grill's bed. "You know how it is. Came into some money. Thought I might buy a little cottage for us out in the woods."

"Us?"

The steaks sizzled. "Nah. Just me."

Morris began to inquire further but couldn't find the words. The heat and the whiskey still had their grip on him with their mind-slurring effects. He didn't know how to proceed, especially when Jack was the shy type, one more likely to observe than engage. And then came another thought: what if the problem was him? It was quite possible that Jack felt intimidated by him. After all, Morris was an outsider among the regular folks on the patio. He reeked of pretentious city life, hand creams and deodorant sprays, busy desk jobs, Chinese takeout, nightclubs, and the very essence of fancy. He was momentarily struck by the idea that here, he was an elite, an honored guest, and people should feel nervous around him.

"Well, I think you're living the dream," Morris said in a moment of haughtiness. "This place is magical. I love it here."

Again, Jack gave a weak smile. In a low voice, he mentioned something indecipherable about Tulsa and home. It was a grim moment, one Morris felt deeply enough to knock away the pedestal he stood upon. He knew with an unearthly premonition that this town probably loved some more than others, and for people like Jack, it took them for granted. *Am I being an asshole?* he wondered.

"Do not ruin those steaks!" Cook yelled out, and they both flinched.

"Maybe you should give me some space," Jack said as the others approached.

"Yes. Of course," Morris replied. "Nice speaking with you."

Soon, he found himself alone and seated as the three continued arguing over the grill. Occasionally, he caught one of them quietly observing him with an appraiser's look as if mentally calculating the worth of each part of him. Even if the afternoon's whiskey hadn't fully settled, he was suddenly eager for another drink. A weak one, at least, enough to prolong that comforting state of giddiness. He lit a cigarette and tried to position himself in the most attractive position possible.

"Excuse me! Do I go ashing all over your living room?" Cook was suddenly at his table, placing an ashtray next to him, letting his other hand stroke his shoulder. Instinctively, Morris leaned into it, surprised to feel the beginnings of an erection. "I just realized you don't have a drink! Let us remedy that." Cook scurried off.

Alone again, he began to feel anxious.

A few moments later, a new figure emerged from the guesthouse. She was a pretty black woman with tightly-knit shoulders and curly hair. Patches of freckles graced her cheeks and nose. She immediately came to his table and placed a plastic tumbler filled to the rim. "Here you go," she said in a calming voice. The drink reeked of booze and juice—perhaps a gin and grapefruit? He did not know, but it smelled dangerous.

"Oh, I shouldn't," he said, trying to push the glass away. Mixing liquors at this stage was never a good idea.

"It's gin-o'clock," she said and helped herself to one of his cigarettes, daintily lit it, and puffed out smoke from her nostrils. "If you don't at least pose with it, they'll be forcing drinks on you all night." Her mouth was curved pleasantly, but it didn't amount to a genuine smile.

Obediently, Morris drank. It was harsh and bitter, and he fought the urge to gag. The woman continued observing him. "Thank you," he said. "It's pretty strong." He took another sip, and this time, it went down smoothly.

"We're having dinner soon."

By the way, she said it, Morris knew she was aware he was already half drunk.

Another sip, and he was doing mental gymnastics, trying to find something to say to her. "I'm sorry. I got pulled into this. I have no idea where I am or what I'm doing here."

This time she did smile. "That's not uncommon."

She was a few years older than him, forty at most, and she possessed a calm, pleasant demeanor. Morris's eyes were drawn to the loud print of her floral shirt and swirls of cherry blossoms under a knitted cardigan. She was dressed in anticipation of cooler weather or to match the inn's ambiance. She reminded him of Yasmin.

But she was turning away towards the grill and losing interest, so he made a business of snubbing out the remains of his cigarette before flinging a hand at her. "I'm Morris. Morris Hines." Why was he being so formal?

Without hesitation, she shook his hand. "Tina," she replied. They were friends now. He drank his drink, and she drank hers, pleasantly nodding at each other as he struggled to compliment the patio as if she owned it.

Soon after, Cook made the production of ringing the dinner bell, and the group assembled as he and Tina brought out trays of food from the guesthouse. The meal was large and oppressive, laid out on every available surface: plates of braised chicken slivers, an imposing green bean casserole over pasta, and crisp bread rolls revealed to have cheese baked inside them, a large plate of peas and onions drizzled in oil. Jack brought over the steaks, his face beaten down with misery. They were overcooked and smoldering, yet Morris graciously took one anyway. The five of them had pooled together at a table that wasn't quite large enough, but it seemed silly for such an intimate party to spread out. Somehow another glass of gin appeared next to him.

Cook and Atherton dominated the conversation for most of the meal, focusing on local gossip or taking small swipes at Jack, who mournfully stared at his plate, cheeks crimson with embarrassment. Tina sometimes laughed politely, occasionally adding some soft wit without drawing attention to herself, or she'd stroke Jack's wrist when he looked most vulnerable. As the meal went on, Morris felt more in possession of himself, though he was too lost to know what anyone was talking about. As early evening approached, the sun lowered, casting a pink shade in the sky. *Such a lovely last evening*, he thought.

"Attention, please." Cook stood and addressed them as if the patio had transformed into his private auditorium. "I hope you are enjoying your dinner, but I do have a few humble words..."

Everyone groaned.

"It's a shame our feast has such few visitors, as we usually have so many here to help us close the season! Why, I look at our little group and wonder where Tony and Lyle and Henry and William are, especially that bitch, Tony. And we must also acknowledge with not-so-great sadness the loss of our dearest Craig, that total slut. May the good people of Des Moines paint blood upon their doors tonight so he'll pass them by with his usual fuckery…"

Tina cleared her throat, and Cook gave her a quick side-eye.

"But I think it's important to recognize our wonderful friends," he went on, "like Jack here. He's like the houseguest who never leaves until one day, you can't imagine life without him."

"Guest or prisoner?" Jack moaned.

"Moving along. I'm delighted that we're still making new friends as well. I hope you enjoy yourself, and we'll see you again." As Cook said this, he winked at Morris, who tensed up in his seat. He did not like the idea of being singled out, but thankfully, Cook moved on. "Now, with the end of the season finally here, it's important to recognize our allied businesses in town…"

Cook's speech faded into white noise as Morris glanced around. He focused on Atherton for a moment, trying to catch his gaze. Between hefty gulps of gin, Cook was prattling on about town politics and ordinances.

"And, of course, what makes us prosperous is the support we receive from our darling benefactors like Atherton here. The Oasis is safe for another year!"

Morris realized Tina and Jack were clapping, so he did the same.

"Are you done yet?" Atherton grumbled.

Cook shut up after that, still smiling, and the meal continued. As they finished, Morris heard a car pulling up and heavy feet storming the entrance. Two middle-aged men appeared, hollering their greetings as they lugged in a cooler.

"You're late," Cook snapped. He downed his drink vengefully and didn't bother to make introductions. No one minded. The group expanded to a second table, poured more gin, and soon they fell again into simultaneous speaking, tossing shady insults at each other and laughing as they did it.

As Morris sat there, focusing on anything said became harder and harder. His mind was foggy and wandering off, down the mountain roads and through the bright lights of downtown, up to the hotel where the resident ghosts were waiting to tuck him into bed.

"I suppose I should get going," he said weakly. No one heard him. He tugged Atherton's sleeve. "I should head out."

Atherton balked. "Where else you gotta be?" When Morris returned a frustrated look, Atherton softened. "It'd be rude to dine and dash. Drink up, and I'll take you back in an hour or so."

Morris found his glass instantly refilled once again. He was fading now, fading off into that mental glaze, the type that he had sought refuge in throughout every family dinner growing up. *Miles away*, his mother would comment. *You're always miles away.* He finished his cocktail; someone complained that the gin was running out. Best have one more before it all turned to whiskey. Another gin. He lit a cigarette as an ache built in his chest—he was smoking too much, but it helped pass the time. After a while, he let his eyes close, and all the voices blurred into a constant unbroken drone—a warm drone like bees, big bees, huge bees on a sweltering day.

A hand grazed him; he straightened up in his seat.

"You're nodding off," Tina said.

He tried to smile, but his muscles rejected the notion. "I'm done for the night."

"Tired already?" The evening had set in, and the sky had bruised into a deep purple. The first few pinpricks of stars appeared overhead. "Maybe you should move around for a bit?" Tina offered. As they rose from their seats, his legs wobbled a bit; he pushed past a head rush and lit another cigarette. "Cook, we're going for a walk," Tina said.

The table went quiet, and now all eyes were scanning over them.

"You know it's getting late," Cook slurred.

"A short one." She cusped Morris's arm.

They walked out from under the pavilion toward one of the paths that led up the hill. It would be pitch black soon, dark enough to swallow them both. There were cabins along the trail, six of them; Morris counted. Each one was large enough to hold a bed and not much else.

Tina was at peace in the evening. Quiet and serene, staring ahead of them with the confidence of a wilderness guide. Eventually, she broke the silence and asked him about Manderlay. "It was marvelous," he kept saying. "Simply marvelous," as he stuttered through a long-winded description of the week's work, trying to talk about his book in a way that did not sound childish.

"What's it about?" she asked.

"It's a fantasy novel."

"I gathered that. But what's the plot?"

He mentally stumbled. "I haven't figured that part out yet." He wondered if he might be making an ass of himself. "Are the cabins open? In case we want to sit down?"

She shook her head.

There was a small plateau in the hillside between cabins four and five. From the vantage point, he could see the full patio and the darkened swimming pool. In the distance, the Christ statue stared out with its fanning arms over the mountain.

"Remember the time…" His voice trailed off. He searched for a story to tell, but one didn't materialize. Tina gave him a soft, amused look with a single raised eyebrow. *What time would we have in common?* he thought. He was shaking off the booze. His stomach felt sour, and he muttered, "You're so quiet."

"It's been a long season. I'm more talkative in the spring."

Below them, the men gossiped on the patio, occasionally erupting in small bursts of laughter. Someone had turned up a radio, and pop music blended into the chorus of their chatter.

"They're debating you right now," she said.

He gave her a confused look. It was all just noise to him. "Can we sit?"

"For a moment, but we shouldn't dawdle. It's getting late. I should have left already."

"Why?"

"Oh, don't be daft." She let go of him, stranded him on his own two legs, and gave a little twirl, accenting her features with ballerina-like gestures. "Because I'm a lady." She curtsied. Her hand extended in wait for a singing bird to perch on it. "At some point, the boys will want to be boys, and I'd be in the way."

Her movements were hypnotic and coy all at once, like Yasmin's.

"What will they do?" he asked. "Once you leave? What will happen?"

Tina let out a small sigh. "I imagine they'll drink more and then go skinny dipping. Maybe a few shenanigans but nothing sinister. Does that bother you?"

"No," he slurred. "I have dabbled in those arts." This didn't seem to surprise or disgust Tina. Her placid expression suggested she had known thisfrom the start. He wondered if he was expected to seduce her, to prove his interest, and at the same time, he wondered if he was still capable; his stomach ached disapprovingly. "I think I need to sit down."

There was a small wooden bench, the boards unhealthy with neglect. As he moved for it, he sensed a slithering motion in the grass, something that was retreating from him. He yelped and stumbled backward and landed on the hard earth.

"There was a snake…"

She lifted a finger to her lips and crawled down next to him. "It's a little late in the season for copperheads. I think you're all right." Then she leaned over him, inspecting him, moving a strand of hair out of his eyes. "We should go back."

Sadness gripped him; he didn't know how to proceed. Everything about her had turned maternal; her smothering concern enveloped him. She was warm-blooded, aided by her cardigan, which drifted over him like a heated blanket. The warmth was starting to settle in a sickening way. Down below, the music kept blaring, but not enough to muffle the occasional laughter. *What are they fucking laughing about?* Tina was saying something again about heading back, but his limbs didn't cooperate. She moved in closer, and the heat in his gut grew stronger until nausea overtook him.

With a sudden jerk, he fell on all fours, crawling away. His stomach convulsed; he vomited. He painfully vomited in abject humiliation, his throat straining, practically tearing itself apart. And then it was over. Somehow, he'd managed to spare his clothes any mess, but his mouth tasted of acid and grime and bile. Not until he felt Tina's hand rubbing circles on his back did he realize he was sobbing.

"I'm so sorry," he mumbled. He felt sober now, painfully so, and weak in the limbs. He spat out whatever yuck was left clinging to his mouth.

"Are you ready?" Tina asked.

"I need some water," he said as her arms cradled him, smelling of sweet lotion, and somehow he was up on his feet, leaning into her as she protected him from falling over again.

How horrid! Had she carried him downhill? He was suddenly approaching the patio again, her arm tenderly wrapped around him as though he were wounded from a fight, his left foot dragging slightly, his head drooped with shame and displeasure. They put him in a chair, propped him up like a marionette, and pulled his strings to feed him water. He greedily drank it down, wanting to drown in it.

"All right, all right. I'm heading out in a minute." Tina turned back to kiss him lightly on the cheek. "You'll be ok."

But she was already fading into the background. As his gaze refocused, all Morris could see was Henry standing there. Henry, dressed in his rags and long sleeves, his fists clenched tightly, observing him. And then, Henry turned away and plopped down at Atherton's table.

"What's he still doing here?" Henry demanded as Atherton contemplated his beer, eyes mellow in the low light, and responded, "I was curious…"

Afterward, only fragments of the night remained:

The men were drunk but not drunk enough.

Henry, at a safe distance. Henry said something to the others while pointing at him.

"Drink this, buddy." More water, cool and cleansing. Cook patted his knee and draped a towel over him. More music.

A white, naked body diving into the pool.

"It's freezing! I'm gonna shrink up into nothing!"

The sounds of cars leaving the lot outside.

Jack's large hand rubbed his back.

"You doin' ok, little buddy?"

The smell of cigar smoke.

Laughter in the distance.

The last thing he remembered was the unnerving quiet when the music died out, the conversations stopped, and the party was long over. He was lying on a pool lounger, curled up against the wind, sweating and cold, somewhere between asleep and awake. He had been here all night, still intact, untouched, and unable to move. He thought he heard Atherton and Cook whispering:

"Another mess you've brought to my table…"

"How was I supposed to know?"

"What am I gonna do with him?"

"He's a big boy. He can figure himself out."

"Maybe we're getting too old for this sort of thing."

"I'll believe it when they quit showing up."

Everything faded to black.

He dreamed.

Chapter 5

During their senior year at Marymount, Morris decided he wanted to go to the National Portrait Gallery. The idea manifested itself after a random conversation about a friend of a friend who recently took a bunch of drugs and toured an art museum. He was eventually escorted out for holding an entire conversation with one of the paintings. The story was ridiculous; Morris didn't believe a word, but soon after, he found himself romanticizing such reckless behavior. He never did hard drugs, nor did he go to museums. It was time to change that. He imagined himself standing in a large marble gallery, gazing out at the shifting patterns of the artwork until he fell into a trance with a single painting. It moved on its own and whispered forbidden knowledge. He was convinced he would have an epiphany.

Of course, Henry latched onto the idea and quickly procured two acid tablets for them. It happened so suddenly that Morris was caught off guard. What had started as a fanciful idea quickly turned into a reality. He was filled with nervous energy in the days leading up to the trip, anxious one moment, near giddy the next, all while knowing Henry would not let him back out.

The tablets looked like tiny opaque windowpanes and left a bitter taste on his tongue that no amount of soda could wash away. As they rode the Metro into the city, he kept looking around, waiting for the euphoria to take him. His patience waned. Aside from a few moments of vertigo and a brief stint of nausea, nothing changed. The world remained at its usual tepid pace, perhaps a little blurry, but still functioned in the usual working order.

In the end, they never made it to the Portrait Gallery but instead went to the Freer and wandered around the ancient Chinese vases. The light made the jades and blues blur like everything was viewed through a thin layer of gauze. There were Asian screens and Hindu statues with their many arms. They stood on the precipice of the Peacock Room and peered inside. The centerpiece portrait, *The Princess from the Land of Porcelain*, glared forward as if she had been waiting for them. The more he stared at her, the more Morris willed himself into believing she had winked. But otherwise, nothing out-of-body occurred, and he was deeply disappointed.

They took a cab to Georgetown Mall because Henry heard there was a cruisy toilet on the top floor. Morris did not want to go. It felt too risky, and that nagging voice was still creeping in, warning that the acid could still take hold at any moment.

"You're in the Tunnel," Henry cooed while wagging a finger.

They loitered inside the men's room for twenty minutes, squatting in stalls, pretending to wash their hands, and giving each other warning looks. Nothing happened. Finally, Morris gave up in favor of browsing CDs at the Sam Goody until he finally dragged Henry down to the food court. They ordered mounds of sushi, coating each piece with wasabi and soy sauce, and Henry chewed more viciously with each bite. There was a mean streak to him, the day's disappointment festering until it oozed out of his pores.

"I'll be back," Henry said and stomped off from their table.

As Morris sat daydreaming, fiddling with his chopsticks, time passed in a slow trickle. He could have sat there forever, picking at the grains of rice left over on his tray, but a security guard eventually knocked on his table and told him to leave. He was startled, if not confused, by the exchange but did as he was told and wandered onto M Street. It was dark out by then, stores lit up, and the headlights of cars came down like a parade of will-o-wisps. Henry had disappeared. As usual.

The morning brought a stabbing pain behind his eyes as if an angry parasite had hatched within his skull and was burrowing outward. Strands of light pierced through tree branches, striking him across the face. The light hurt. His back hurt. Every part of him hurt. As he twisted onto his side and pulled his blanket around him, the world finally became focused. He was outdoors, pressed against the hard bands of a pool lounger, clutching not a blanket but a towel, a scratchy beach towel barely large enough to cover him. A figure moved in the distance, a hazy blur of movement, but it was nothing more than a feral cat lunging at some unseen prey. Then, with a jerk, he shot up and stared out over the patio. He was at the Oasis, and he was alone.

The previous night came to him in a series of distorted images, a slideshow with the static of an archaic TV screen. He mentally adjusted the antenna to see them more clearly. There had been the lost, hazy feeling on the patio, surrounded by overlapping conversations and endless gin cocktails and the grandiose meal. He could picture Tina's face, serene and warm, and their walk up the hill where he almost vomited on her. Then there was the descent. He had glimpses of the rest of the night, drifting off on top of the lounger, interrupted when people came to check on him. He had seen men drink, laugh, dive naked into the pool, clammer about and finally disappear. He had watched it all in a state of drunken half-sleep, and it was hard to parse out what was real and what was imagined.

First, you take a drink, and then the drink takes a drink, and then the drink takes you. Someone famous said that; he was certain.

Eventually, he forced himself to move, willing himself to rise off the lounger, his movements rigid and zombie-like; he slowly made his way to the outdoor kitchen and drank straight from the faucet, ignoring the metallic taste, until he will full, no, bloated with water. But it was good. Life renewed in him, and the stabbing pain behind his eyes subsided as his limbs loosened. On one of the nearby tables, he found a discarded pack of Marlboros. With the first cigarette, he began to feel more like himself again. He finished another and wandered over to the grassy knoll, staring upward at the little cottages above and pissed. The breeze had died down, and it was turning into a pleasant morning, the trees colorful and artfully shrouding the cottages. It was a gorgeous scene, and he took out his phone to take a picture.

It was almost half past eight. So early and yet...

His plane! *Fuck!* His plane departed at ten, and he was standing there, dick out, ready to photograph the landscape. He was instantly winded and, in a panic, rushed along the patio to grab his things, but then remembered his bags were waiting for him at the hotel. He would need to call a cab, but he didn't know the number or the address of where he was. He brought up the map on his phone, but his mind was spiraling all over the place. He should call an Uber, except in a town this small, there weren't any. Should he call the hotel instead? *Why? Why would I call them?* And then, he stood there, paralyzed with indecision, before realizing none of it mattered. There wasn't enough time. It was a sickening thought, a quick stab in the gut, and his life was spilling out of him. He would lose his job over this; his years of quiet, determined work were all undone. And then, Yasmin, stony-faced Yasmin, came to mind. He pictured her at the airport baggage claim, sitting quietly, reading her book, pausing only to glance about with deadly silence. She would check her phone once and then calmly rise and leave.

He couldn't bare the idea of facing her, much less speaking to her now. He was constantly fucking up. He was always procrastinating, forgetting details, squandering money, screwing up the manifests at work, and destroying the kitchen and the bathroom. His heart thumped so painfully that he thought he might have a spectacular heart attack. With a bit of luck, he'd be confined to bed under a doctor's care or maybe even die. At least then, there would be a reason.

Atherton. The name struck a bell and ranged viciously. Atherton, with his haughty mutton-chopped grizzled smirk. Atherton, who had encouraged him to stay and was supposed to take him back. This man had lured him away from town and placed him in the middle of chaos with the same indifference of moving a pawn into the Queen's path. Morris let out a low groan, his fists clenched to expose the white of his knuckles. This was all Atherton's fault. He should have known better than to trust him. After all, a psychic had once warned him against all unnecessary travel, that a demon was in his future and his game was sabotage.

The bitter quiet was disrupted by the drawn-out creak of a door opening, that wheezing ear-splitting noise that made an entrance more dramatic. Morris turned to find His Majesty Cook waltzing out onto the patio, wrapped in his royal bathrobe. The scene was almost comical as Cook paraded out, holding his coffee mug like a scepter, his robe parting just enough to reveal the royal pouch snug in his briefs. Any other morning, Morris would have imagined seventies porn music playing in the background.

"You are a mess," Cook said. His voice oozed like honey over an open wound, attracting flies. "Hungover?"

"Where's Atherton?" he snapped.

Cook blanched. "Probably at home. Or maybe out at work. Are you all right?"

"No. He was supposed to take me back."

"No worries. I can take you back whenever."

"No! Everything is fucked up, and Atherton shouldn't have left me here!" He rose out of his chair and began to pace. His face flushed red hot.

"Relax. You're fine. It's still early—hotel checkouts aren't for a few hours."

"That's not the point!" Morris screamed. He was on fire now, spitting out words to extinguish it, though he wasn't sure exactly what he was screaming about. There were curses against Atherton and the Oasis and yelling about his plane, all while Cook stood in silence, face calm and blank until Morris finally fizzled out.

"Calm down, please," Cook said. He looked overwhelmed. "When is your plane?"

"I don't know—in an hour?"

Cook looked stunned as if he'd slammed into an invisible wall. "Why would you go out drinking if you had an early flight?"

"I didn't plan it. But I trusted you all to get me back." He flung a finger forward in accusation. "This is your fault!"

"Enough!" Cook's voice shot out like a pistol and ricocheted off the surrounding ridge, booming with such anger that Morris froze in place. "Sit down and shut up."

The fire inside him abruptly extinguished without so much as a burning ember left. Then came the drop as he obediently sat on the nearest lounger and watched Cook calmly return inside the guesthouse. Alone again, the previous moments replayed in his mind with mortifying repetition. He shuddered as he saw himself wailing like a bratty teenager, making accusations against the only man available to take him back to town. Cook was probably inside, waiting patiently for him to leave alone. Another terrible image came to mind: he begged Cook to help him, clinging to his leg like a serf. *Please take me back. Please don't kick me out like this.* It was even more undignified.

But eventually, Cook did return with an uncapped beer bottle and some aspirin tablets. One quick sigh and the veil of hospitality was back on his face. He smiled. "This will make you feel better," and he presented his offerings.

"You don't hate me?" Morris asked weakly.

Cook stifled a laugh. "You're hungover."

In truth, Morris didn't feel all that terrible, but it seemed a good idea to feign as much pain as possible. "May I have some water instead?" Morris did his best to make his voice go coarse as gravel.

"Beer first. Hair of the dog. Trust me."

The beer was warm and bitter and pooled sickeningly in his stomach. He took the aspirin even though he didn't need them.

"I let the beer go flat. It's better that way when you feel the way you do." Water was next. Then coffee. They sat together at one of the little tables, Cook observing him with an amused expression. "Are you feeling better?"

"Slightly." He felt more vulnerable than anything. "I'm sorry about earlier."

But Cook waved off the last comment with a flick of his wrist. "Why don't we focus on the current situation? What do you gotta do now?"

Again, he was taken aback. He was not used to being dismissed so quickly. "Ok. Well, I suppose I need a new flight."

"Good start. Call them up now. Tell them you have a stomach bug. You're throwing up. Appeal to their sympathy. See what they can do."

Morris paced along the patio for half an hour, forcing a pained, tortured voice as he spoke to the agent. He was so sick, he claimed. He couldn't possibly travel, and he'd already missed his previous flight and wasn't sure he could afford another. A manager took pity on him and gave him credit. He could book a new flight as soon as he was well again. When he hung up, he returned to the table and lit another cigarette as Cook applauded him.

"Well done. Now, what's next?"

"My job. They're going to fire me. I know it."

"Oh, please. You have an excuse, so you might as well use it. Tell it to your fiancé, too. People get sick. Oh, tell them you ate bad clams at Hobos Restaurant. I hate those bitches." With that, Cook waved his hand as if the matter was settled. "Feel better?"

"All I need now is a place to crash until I can fly home," Morris said.

"Don't press your luck. Last night was a freebee."

Morris leaned back in a stupor, his body melding into his chair as a sense of relief washed over him. It was that simple. No catastrophe; no crisis. Only stillness. They sat quietly, sipping their coffee. It was so early. Now, there was no need to rush. "Thank you," he finally said; his voice went soft and pliable. It could be bent from all angles. "Thank you for everything."

Cook shrugged. He retrieved a tarnished cistern and refilled their coffees.

"So, what did I miss last night? I can barely remember anything."

"Oh please, I don't believe that for one bit. If you can't remember it, then it didn't happen." There was a savage undertone in Cook's voice as if he were suddenly ready to quell him into an argument. "Dearheart, the most interesting thing you did last night was disappear with Tina for a bit. Everyone was speculating over it. I predict that if you weren't so messy, she would have taken you home, and then you would be her problem."

"Nothing happened."

Cook's eyebrow rose in a dramatic arch. "Are you sure? Because Tina will tell me everything."

"I almost threw up on her," Morris blurted out, and Cook erupted in a hefty laugh.

"You really are a prize!" He was enjoying himself now. "Oh, Tina! Isn't she amazing? She's what we call one of the town peacocks. Not as flashy as some, but she's got that spark. And she's very picky. You screwed that one up, didn't you?"

The subject of Tina was like a blister ready to pop; he avoided touching it. "Henry was here last night as well, wasn't he?"

"Oh, yeh, Atherton told me all about that. Wasn't as entertaining as I'd hoped." Cook lit a cigarette and sucked it down with the intensity of a lover.

"He seemed really angry. Was it because I was here?"

"Oh, Henry needs to get over himself," Cook said with deviltry. "His best asset was being a new pretty face. That was years ago. He's no longer new, he's no longer pretty, and quite frankly, he's high maintenance. He needs to realize he's not interesting enough to be high maintenance." Again, he refilled their coffees. "Unlike Tina. She's not high maintenance, she's very pretty, and she's very, very interesting."

Morris glanced at the pool and saw ripples from the previous night. Phantom bodies stripped, swam, and splashed like happy children. And he had been stuck on the side, impotent with drink, unable to join them. Part of him wanted to rectify that now, to shut off this conversation by stripping down and diving in. But he didn't. He sat there imagining what could have happened.

Cook continued. "Tina's a potent creature. Very sexual. Now, if I had to conform and settle down, I'd want someone like her. Tina likes sex, likes to experiment, and likes variety. She's also very prudent. She's cautious with whom she confides. We'd make a great couple. We'd do whoever we like and then would have marvelous stories to share in the morning." The lines on his mouth arched up into something wicked. "As you can see, we love having her around. She helps us weed 'em out."

"She sounds like my Yasmin," Morris said.

"You have a type."

"Not really. I like variety." He chose his words carefully. "I have a masochistic need to try new things."

Cook gave him another dry look, his brow furrowed as if he were mentally dissecting him. "I don't know what that means."

They made small talk for a little longer, about Tina, about the Oasis and its long roster of married men who came each summer to escape their lives. When Morris finally found the courage to ask about a swim, Cook shook his head. He had turned the heater off the night before; now, the water was far too cold.

"I suppose it's time to head out. Gotta get you back."

"I think I might stay a few extra days," Morris mused.

"That's how it begins." Cook was already picking up the dishes. "You be careful, or you'll end like Henry. Or worse, Jack." He disappeared into the guesthouse and emerged fully dressed, twirling car keys around his finger. "All right, get up. Breakfast is reserved for paying customers only."

He felt pulled by the collar outside and around where Cook's faded sedan waited for them. They drove along the wooded roads that led toward the empty neighborhoods. "You've picked a bad time of year to get yourself stranded," Cook said. "Town's mostly dead during the week. A few places stay open. The Cider Mill never closes…" They took a roundabout way and entered on the opposite end of town, pausing in front of a square brick building with a faded sign: "Accounting Services" printed over the entranceway. "Just so you know, Ms. Tina works there, in case you wanted to stop in and say hi."

"I might use the next few days for writing," Morris said.

"Good idea," Cook replied but offered nothing else.

They idled in front of the Stoney Brook Hotel. As Morris stepped out, the wind whistled, striking up a chorus of chimes dangling from a nearby storefront. A woman passed by, giving a courteous nod; the park foundation gurgled proudly. He turned back to Cook, toying with the idea of inviting him inside, but then thought better of it.

"One bit of advice," Cook said. "Don't go messing with Atherton. Let that be."

Morris frowned. "Well, I still have a bone to pick with him."

"Don't. I mean it. Finish eating what you got first before you go adding shit to your plate."

"Right. Thanks." And then, the urge took him. "Maybe I'll see you around?" he asked.

"Maybe," Cook said and twiddled his fingers goodbye.

He watched Cook drive off and vanish down the road until he was left with a slight pang of rejection. Perhaps the morning would have ended differently if he had been bolder and had made his intentions known. *Let me thank you for your hospitality.* Funny how you wanted something most when it was no longer available, even when you hadn't seen the appeal from the start. He still had the urge to swim. It didn't matter. Cook was gone, and he was on his own again. There would be other opportunities, endless time to fill, empty time to spend like a bottomless purse of coins.

There were things to do. He would need to extend his stay at the hotel. His laptop waited for him on the Victorian claw-footed desk. He would email work and tell them of his illness—some vague combinations of symptoms, enough for them to assume the worst and not ask too many questions. Then, he'd email Yasmin and give her the same story with a flurry of apologies. And she would buy enough of it to at least pretend she was not suspicious. Then, he would chug water and plunge himself onto the bed, immerse himself in the floral patterns of the duvet, that absurd grid of poppies, and sleep off any residue from the night before. He'd write and drink and live deliciously, even if only for an extra day or two. And when he was ready, he'd go home with a new sense of purpose.

But first, food. It was the essential thing.

Up and around the corner, he chose a small, miraculously open bakery. It was a yawning brown café that mixed dark nutritious wood, cheap Formica counters, tin ceiling tiles, little high tea displays, and lacy things that didn't belong there. Whatever this space was, it seemed forced against its will to be a coffee bar. Morris took a seat at the table nearest the front window and waited patiently until he realized he had to go up to order.

Behind the counter stood a youngish woman dressed in her baker fatigues, with dark, dark makeup and dreadlocked hair tied behind her in an imposing bundle. She was so out of place, a punk-rock diva with the serene smile of a kindergarten teacher. The menu wasn't extensive or impressive, but there were treats on display. For lunch, he settled on meringue-topped pastries. "Okay, but they're from yesterday," the woman said as a warning. She brought them with coffee served in a chipped teacup and a small biscuit at his table.

What kind of a man eats meringues for lunch? He was staring at them and grinning monstrously. An eccentric, an artist, someone who's unconventional. That was who he was now. There were three meringues on his plate, all blossoms begging to be eaten. The baker gave him an incredulous look as if she were spying on a greedy child, but he didn't care. He was performing for her now: his face sadistically childlike as he smashed the first meringue with his fork and red cream oozed out from the bottom. Outside, the little town sat in its sleepy isolation, with its pastel awnings, cobblestone terraces, ghosts, and decadent poverty. "I have wasted my life," he said out loud to no one in particular.

From behind the counter, the baker giggled.

Chapter 6

What was there to do in a small town during the off-season? A surprising amount, really. The mornings began along the River Walk, breathing in the faint smells of earth and mold, waltzing by the vacant restaurant patios. He imagined the height of summer, the flowerbeds in full bloom, the patios full of haughty waiters who carried plates of smoked salmon and quiche. He spent an hour in the Stillwater Bath House, sitting in a claw foot tub filled with rose water, and later attended a ghost tour at the Abernathy Manor and took selfies with the twin mermaid statues outside the library. One afternoon, he sat alone in the sculpture garden watching the shadows move with the receding sunlight. He smoked three cigarettes until he blew the perfect smoke ring. An hour passed, during which he barely thought of anything and wondered if this was what meditation felt like.

He drank nothing but whiskey. Whiskey on the rocks, whiskey and water, whiskey sours until he was confident his blood was the color of brown liquor. And when there was no whiskey, he drank beer. Cold frothy-headed beer, enough to make his belly swell with a giant gas bubble. He'd start early when the bars were accepting orders, just a shot to get it started and then another to prolong the lightheaded buzzing. He chain-smoked cigarettes until his throat was raw. He masturbated in public restrooms with furious dry strokes that almost broke the skin. And then, he went skipping down the street, harboring a wonderful secret.

After a day, his clothes began to stink. His face was changing, too. It looked more angular and prickly with wayward whiskers until his reflection revealed a darling vagabond. At a consignment shop, he bought two billowy Panama shirts, a pair of brown linen pants, and a cardigan jacket for the chilly nights—all reasonably priced, almost as good as theft. To complete the ensemble, he added a string of wooden beads around his neck and felt deliciously bohemian strutting down the streets.

He did not return to the Oasis, even though he tried. He loitered in the Public House, hoping it would lead to someone familiar. It never did. Instead, he looked for new ways to get into trouble and sniffed out the company of strangers. He drank steadily; he got bold. He bought a drink for the wrong type of man and left before he was chased out. It was a little reminder that the world was what it was, not where he wished it to be. That night, he collapsed onto his bed, felt the weight of drink upon him, too tired to even jerk off, and fell asleep thinking, *One more day to get it right.*

In the stink of the afternoon, he escaped the sun-soaked streets and entered the taut brick building of the tax office, where he managed to finagle his way past the receptionist and into Tina's office. She sat patiently behind her desk, smiling sweetly, though it was apparent that neither one knew precisely what to say. He was trying to think of an invitation for her, a lure of sorts, though soon it was apparent he was fishing with an empty hook. She was working; she did not have time to play. But she very much enjoyed the visit, she assured him. Eventually, she wrote her phone number on a scrap of paper. "Another time," she said sweetly. He folded it up and placed it among the receipts in his wallet, where he promptly forgot about it.

Midweek and it began to rain. Thunderstorms rolled through, battering downtown like something biblical. It was his first day trapped inside the hotel, idling between his room and the dining hall balcony that overlooked the park. It felt like penance. He began to wonder if he'd outstayed his welcome.

Yasmin sent him an email. "When you are back, we should talk." A simple assertion, nothing remarkable about it. There were no questions about his whereabouts or his return date, just the blunt understanding that he was gone, he would come home, and there would be a discussion—no emotion, no judgment, very pointedly Yasmin. The rest of the email was dedicated to the happenings back at home. In short but fluid prose, she described the comings and goings of their friends. Work kept her busy, but the previous night, she attended a Caryl Churchill play at the Studio Theater, which started in the 1800s, but the second act moved to the 1970s even though the characters had only aged a few years. She was writing a piece on it and wished he was there to help her with it in one last act of sentimentality.

Before Yasmin submitted any of her articles for publication, she would have Morris read them out loud. One of her many side projects was writing theater reviews for various magazines and websites that only paid a little but usually supplied free tickets. They would sit together around the dinette with a bottle of Merlot (their theater wine), and Yasmin would take notes as he read—sometimes carving out entire paragraphs she found superfluous. It was a tedious process: she haggled with him over word choices and sometimes needed to hear variations of the same sentence read over and over again. Many reviews revealed her eye for aesthetics and attention to props and lighting; her favorite word was "minimalist." Over time, this ritual had a profound effect on him. When he attended the plays, he nursed a newfound awareness of the set, where the actors stood in relation to each other, and was constantly aware of dark space.

But a different side of Yasmin revealed itself on those nights out at the theater. She only ate or drank something in the hours before they arrived. If Morris treated himself to a glass of wine in the bar, she would only sip a bit of water and toss the bottle away before they took their seats. Her face was different as well. Usually, it was smooth and expressionless, but in the dark, her brow was always creased, and her lips parted as if she were on the verge of a gasp. She would hold his hand tightly from the curtain until intermission and be untouchable throughout the second act. When the cast assembled to bow, her face was lost in another world, eyes wide and mystified. But the moment they stepped back onto the street, the whimsy would fade as she reverted to her normal state of detachment, guarding her emotions, and would only offer very technical opinions. As jarring as these transitions were, they were most endearing. They were the moments when he could see past the veneer and glimpse her secret self.

How strange that he should think of her now when, through the prior days, she had all but vanished from his mind. He loved her, but he did not long for her. He could only see and feel the present moment. That was the sign that told him he needed to return home, that if he were gone too long, he would forget what he loved most about it.

By sundown, the rain finally stopped, and a thick mist moved over downtown, like in the best of mystery stories. Again, the streets beckoned. He was hungry and restless and ready for one last drink. Such a shame to waste so much time without sampling the entire buffet. Another night would not make a difference. He assured himself that tomorrow he would resolve everything and return home. But this last night was his. He showered and dressed and went out to meet it.

Chapter 7

They only sang the old songs. The new songs didn't work here; they were all glitz and sparkle and demanded too much attention, unlike the old songs, which were content and unpretentious. They were everyone's darling uncle, the one who drank too much, who knew the meaning of a hard day's work, who told too many stories and only cursed when he thought the parents weren't listening. That was how the old songs worked. They beckoned in you in close and offered you a bit of wisdom, and before you knew it, you were singing along.

Morris sat in the back corner of a karaoke bar, an underground space that created the idea of a bomb shelter turned bootleg. The cellar bar was mostly empty except for the handful of performers crowded together, each taking their turn butchering the classics. Each one was worse than the last. Two willowy men struggled their way through Van Halen with slurred voices. They were followed by a frumpy middle-aged woman who gave a wailing version of "Ring of Fire." With each new singer, Morris considered leaving, except there was nowhere else to go.

He drank beer straight from the bottle and made small talk with the man next to him. Will was a soft-spoken older fellow who observed the singers with a sense of lethargy, eyes too glazed over to wince at an off-key pitch. They had gravitated towards each other with their subtle dance of sideways glances and nods until conversation felt unavoidable. From their vantage point, they had the camaraderie of gawking wallflowers. All the singers were drunk and terrible and provided endless amusement.

"Usually, she does a decent Tammy Wynette." Will pointed to the most recent singer. "When she's sober, she ain't bad. She's not good, but not terrible."

"I'll take your word for it," Morris replied.

They clinked their drinks and fell into the safe banter of the bands they liked. It was not the conversation he was looking for, but Morris played along. He mentioned his enduring favorites from the morning commute: the Flaming Lips, My Morning Jacket, Florence + The Machine. Simply listing their names made him feel pretentious. What kind of a group calls themselves Arcade Fire? Only the best, though Will didn't seem to agree. He preferred the old ballads and simple names: Johnny Cash, Simon & Garfunkle, and Janis Joplin, though his heart belonged to Tammy Wynette.

"Tammy's greatest hits were 'Divorce' and 'Stand by Your Man.' Is that irony or an oxymoron?" Will said, and Morris smiled awkwardly.

Another singer strained over Sarah McLaughlin, and when she finished, Will gave a soft applause.

"No, don't clap," Morris said. "Don't encourage them."

There was a short lull in the music as the next singer approached the stage. She was a frail elderly woman, her face brightly painted up like a lost performer of the *Moulin Rouge*. The familiar chords of "Landslide" started over the speakers as a few onlookers hollered. And then she was singing, voice smooth as dark molasses, draping her bedazzled cardigan over her shoulders as if it were one of Stevie Nicks' shawls.

Morris leaned in and whispered, "I used to steal my parents' records and stayed up all night listening to them. Fleetwood Mac was one of my favorites. I'd pretend I was Lindsey Buckingham giving a concert in my bedroom."

This wasn't true. His parents never listened to Fleetwood Mac, at least not that he could remember, and he could only recognize one or two of their songs. He wasn't sure why he said it.

"I like the old stuff," he added.

Will's brow creased as he nodded. "Yeah, I suppose Fleetwood Mac is old."

"It's not old people's music! It's just older music." This time, Will gave him an incredulous look, and Morris downed the rest of his beer. "Sorry. I don't know what I'm saying."

The music stopped, and the frail little singer curtsied to the applause of her modest little audience. Against his better judgment, Morris found himself clapping as well. She was the best singer so far. As she descended the stage, her gaze shot forward, finally noticing the two wallflowers, and she glided across the room as if drawn to them. Up close, she looked even more fragile, her face crinkling under heavy mounds of makeup. *One of the town peacocks,* Morris thought.

"You two are mighty cozy back here," she exclaimed and, without hesitation, wedged herself between them, lassoing them with what Morris imagined as an invisible feather boa. "My name is Sharon, but everyone here calls me Sharona. Now, when are you two singing?"

There was a drunken quality to all her mannerisms, not so much as intoxicated but uninhibited. She spoke in slurred sentences, complimenting them one minute and then demanding answers to unasked questions the next as she draped her bony arms affectionately around them. Morris struggled to conceal his discomfort. Sharona was harmless but crazy, and he did not want any of her painted face to rub off on him.

"And you...you're not from here at all," she finally said with authority. She grasped him, palpitating his arm with her little soft claws. Morris smiled and shrugged and feigned shyness, and she leeched it up. "Give me your palm," she ordered, then traced up and down his lifeline, digging her nail in as though she were trying to draw blood. "You're a lost soul," she said. "You move around constantly. You have no idea what you want in life. You've already had two failed businesses, and you'll have a third before you're able to settle down."

He tried to pull his hand away, but she held on tight. *Jesus, when was the last time she washed her hands?*

"You have to give up your technology. You're addicted to it, and that's the only way you'll be able to embrace your full potential. And don't worry about your failed marriage. You aren't meant for just one person."

She then released him, satisfied with the gifts she had given.

"That was surprisingly accurate," Morris said through clenched teeth as Will chuckled.

Then, Sharona gave them both a hard up and down look as if she were genuinely seeing them for the first time. "Oh, but I shouldn't have interrupted you!" she exclaimed. "A fair warning for you both: there's trouble brewing in these hills. Terrible things are on the horizon; best be prepared. Buy everything you can: shampoo, cans, soap, whatever. You'll need it to barter. We've gone through tough times, but I'm afraid it's only getting worse. Men like you will have it the toughest, I'm afraid." And then she fluttered away back towards the stage.

They sat there glowing in the aftermath of Sharona's prophecy. *Men like you.* Morris clung to that remark. She didn't know him. "What a lunatic," he finally said. "I hope that wasn't too weird."

"Not at all. I quite enjoyed it." Will folded his hands like a bishop, almost praying for inspiration. "Well, if Armageddon is so close, we should have another beverage."

Morris let a coy smile creep upon his lips. "I'm not sure if I should. Supposedly, I'm leaving in the morning."

"Supposedly?"

"I should have left days ago, but I keep prolonging my trip." He felt that familiar tingling in his gut, eating up such focused attention. He had not imagined sleeping with Will, nor was he confident he'd enjoy it. Still, without other prospects nearby, he was becoming more amenable to the idea, and a free drink was always appreciated.

"Come on. I'll get us another round, and then, if you want, we can take a walk."

Will's hand dropped down to where his jacket hung on its peg as if to fish something out of its pocket. At the same time, Morris felt him brush against his leg, a quick caress of his calf, and then grazing against his knee. It all occurred in one unexpected moment, and Morris jerked back, his stool loudly scraping against the floorboards with such a sound that it startled them both. It was unintentional, a series of simple reflexes that ended with both in defensive positions. Will clutched his hand as if it were bitten.

"Sorry." His brow creased, and then he turned away, half-hunched over the bar. "My mistake. I thought I recognized something in you."

Morris, however, had not moved. He still sat on his barstool, both knees bent as if practically begging hands to rest on them. He could not decipher why he had violently jerked away from him or why it mattered. As he stared forward at Will's profile, he felt an invisible barrier erect between them. "I'm sorry about that," he said in a nervous voice, though Will was now typing into his phone and didn't seem to hear him. Their camaraderie was gone, and now they were strangers again. *You did recognize something*, he thought. *It's there, but it's out of practice.*

When the bartender finally approached, Will ordered himself another cocktail.

What about mine?

The bar continued in its usual mechanisms as performers rotated in their unharmonious cycle. The music was getting worse: off-key, slurred voices cracking under the weight of their chords. Morris sat quietly for a long time, cupping his beer bottle and scuffling it across the bar top as if to prove it was still empty. Will stared into his phone, its glow casting him in an eerie halo. He was now in his private world, where nothing else seemed to exist. Reluctantly, Morris ordered himself another beer. He tried to arrange his body into the least repulsive configuration possible. He sucked in his gut and extended his neck. His discomfort mounted.

"When are you going to sing?" he asked. Will didn't respond but instead gave a quick side-glance and a shrug and continued to sink further away as if to cut off any further contact. Morris began to feel depressed. "Last night in town," he muttered to no response. He bit his underlip, tasted nothing but bitterness, and sipped it down with bitter beer. He wondered if the rain had started again—there were no windows in this cacophonic cave. But to go out and check, leaving his seat even for a moment, signified an ending. And it was late. Not late in hours, but late in energy. There were other bars, but at this stage of the night, drinkers had passed their peak and were close to tempering out. It was too late to start over.

One more try. And then I'll go.

He impulsively tapped Will on the shoulder but instantly regretted it. He had nothing planned to say, and the whole act felt like a childish cry for attention.

Will looked at him curiously. "What time does this place shut down?"

"Why? I thought you were leaving."

That was such a cold reply, Morris flushed cherry red. "Sorry," he muttered and focused back on his beer, nursing his embarrassment as he debated getting up and moving to a table. If Yasmin had been there, she would have shot back without hesitation. *Well, I thought you were going to buy me a drink.* Or maybe she'd be more direct. *I am going, apparently, by myself.* Of course, Yasmin wouldn't have said that. She was too proud to let someone reject her. And then, Morris wondered what he was still doing there and what had been so appealing about Will in the first place. In the distance, a pot-bellied man rose to the stage and began a murderous version of Jim Croce. Now seemed like a perfect time to retreat to the hotel, pack up, and masturbate himself to sleep.

"They usually shut down when the singing stops. They'll tire themselves out soon enough." Will downed the rest of his cocktail and paid his tab.

From across the bar, a new figure approached, a huge swollen man rosy-cheeked and beady eyes; everything about him conjured the image of sweat. He saddled up next to Will and pulled him into a half-hug greeting. "Ready to go?" he asked in a surprisingly meek voice. And then, he glanced at Morris with a quip of astonishment.

"Hi, Jack," Morris said.

"Hey, buddy!" Jack's face beamed. "I thought you left."

"I was delayed," Morris said and stood up to properly greet him but was caught off guard when Jack hugged him. He felt himself sink deeply into his embrace until he was almost swallowed up.

Will seemed less amused. His fingers tapped impatiently against the bar top. "I'm ready when you are."

"Where are we going?" Morris asked, much to Will's dismay.

"The Oasis," Jack said with a shrug as if there were no place else.

The Oasis, where grown men went to play like children. Hope renewed; the night might still be salvaged. A skeptical look fell over Will's face, making the prospect of it all more appealing.

"Wonderful," Morris said. "I was hoping to see Cook one last time before I leave."

And then it was settled. They were going to the Oasis. Outside, it was late and dark, and the air held the chilly grasp of Autumn. Morris was thankful for his cardigan and pulled it tight around him as he squatted in the backseat of Jack's sedan. They rolled down the windows to smoke as they drove through the wood-lined roads out of town. There was the moon, still obscured by storm clouds, and the bright beacon of the Jesus statue staring out from its ridge. Soon, they were in the parking lot of The Oasis, walking through the front gate, and onto the darkened patio.

In the dim light, Morris made out the shape of Cook sitting under one of the table umbrellas, his head tilted back, eyes closed, and mouth parted as if caught in a yawn. There were subtle movements, his thick body rocking and swaying. As Morris's eyes adjusted, the image became complete. There was another person, crouched low, head bobbing up and down in Cook's lap. Instantly, Morris felt his stomach seize up with that sense of trespass, though he could not look away.

"Nice night for it," Will said.

"Yup." Cook smiled. As he opened his eyes, he released a little gasp. "What the hell are you still doing here?"

Henry lifted his head and lazily peered around. He did not seem bothered by the intrusion until he recognized Morris's horrified stare. Only then did Henry curse, his face contorted into something feral before he darted off towards the dining pavilion. No one was fazed by this, even as Cook's chubby dick pointed forward at them like a diving rod. He took his time pulling up his shorts as Will and Jack nodded to each other as if to say, *Oops! Sorry about that. Isn't this funny?*

"I'm grabbing a beer," Henry called out from the shadows.

"Get in the shower first!" Cook snapped. There was a small protest, which Cook instantly squashed. "No, you greasy mutt! Take a damn shower!" He shook his head and rolled his eyes with an exasperated flair.

Morris was still frozen in place.

"Stop gawking. You can't be offended by shit left in the toilet when you show up unannounced." Cook's voice was haughty and thick as curdled milk. He practically gargled. "You need wine."

"Oh, I shouldn't." Morris fell back into his coy ways and smiled sweetly as he did it.

"But you will." And then Cook trotted off into the guesthouse. Even inside, his voice erupted. "Stop procrastinating and take a goddamn shower!"

Within moments, they huddled together against the breeze, seated around the metal patio table in the near darkness. Merlot was poured into plastic goblets. They all exhaled the brisk night under the careful watch of changing trees, the stars, and the omnipresent statue. Oh, that strange beacon, how he had forgotten about it until now that it was looming above, illuminated by spotlights so that one could not help but feel its gloating presence, the tall and silent voyeur.

Morris took a sip and then another sip. Cook and Will had fallen into deep conversation, discussing their businesses in the droll tone of work, that killer of pleasure. Morris could not break in with a single word and drank his irritation until his glass was refilled. He had not come to drink and talk but to do and act. He was now hungry to do anything.

"Don't mind 'em. They're old friends," Jack whispered. Poor quiet Jack. Of the three, he was the last one Morris hoped to be saddled up to. Jack's hunger was different. He might crave meat but seemed equally content with a bit of bread and butter.

"You're their friend, too." As Morris said this, his mind trailed off. The whole scene came into focus: the dark patio, the creeping cold, the endless wine, all of them waiting while Henry bathed inside. They were all waiting for Henry. Dear Lord. *Why am I here?* Jack was still talking to him in slow, measured beats that were dull down to the chord; Morris faintly nodded to give the impression he was listening. *This is what people do here. They sit and talk and drink and wait.*

"I'm sorry I'm boring you," Jack said funereally.

Yanked back into the moment, Morris stammered. "Oh no. It's not you—I have a terrible habit of spacing out every now and then." He forced a reassuring smile. It was a shame he did not like Jack more than he did; nice people deserved to be cared for.

The entire table went quiet as the guesthouse door opened. Henry haughtily wandered out, freshly bathed and primed, lips pouting, eyes shiny as glass. He looked almost translucent in the night, his shirt billowing around him.

"I'm feeling a bit tired, so I'm gonna head out," he said.

Cook's mouth gaped open into a horrified *O*. He looked offended. "Are you shitting me? It'll start storming again any minute! You'll get swept away, and by the time we find your body, it'll be too late for an open casket." He rose and filled the fifth glass with wine; they were on their second bottle, which was now empty. Before there was any protest, Cook thrust the goblet at Henry. "You can shack up with me."

The wind picked up again. Goosebumps sprinkled onto their arms as a distant rumbling echoed off the hills. Sips of wine became whole mouthfuls.

It was Cook who again broke the silence. He turned to Will and made a grand sweeping gesture towards the rest of the table. "So, Henry and Morris here are actually old high school buddies. Haven't seen each other in years and magically ran into each other downtown…" From there, Cook gave his own retelling of that night, that fateful night of the blackout, with the confidence of someone who had been there. Cook often bore witness to events he had no part in, but his word was Gospel. Will nodded, though he did not seem impressed with the story.

Eventually, Morris interjected. "We met in college," he said, feeling all eyes fall upon him with great expectation. "At Marymount."

The whole group was now looking at him, and Morris started to regret speaking up. His mind had gone fuzzy from all the drinks; focusing on one single thread of thought was difficult.

Cook let out a little chirp. "College? You actually went to college?"

"Stop it," Henry muttered.

"Oh, you're no fun tonight," Will said between cigarettes. "I want the full backstory."

Jack started to giggle. "I hope it's a romance story."

Cook grunted with a roll of his eyes. "A gothic romance at best." He collected the empty wine bottles and returned inside to fetch a third.

"Hardly," Morris called out after him. "We were friends. Close friends." There was a little slur to his speech, but no one seemed to notice.

"We got it. Special friends," Will said, smirking into his glass.

"Look, I'm trying to be serious." The wine was taking hold now, and he could feel a slight delay between his thoughts and the words that came out of his mouth. Still, Morris persisted. "Friendship is a thing, right? It's specific and meaningful, even if it's one-sided. And even when it ends, it's still a part of your history." He was stumbling down a mental stairwell, rambling with each step. He felt compelled to explain all of it: those tender college years and the years afterward, even as Henry sat in a grimacing silence. "Come on, Jack. You get it, right?"

Will took Jack's turn. "Stay focused. What happened? How did it end?"

"Can we change the subject?" Henry snapped, and everyone stared.

"What if we just talked about the good parts," Morris said. He saw Henry now through that delightful lens of nostalgia. It disarmed him. Years of anger, grief, loathing, and confusion were instantly defused and replaced with a desire for peace.

"I don't remember the good parts," Henry said. He was building walls, trying to stay just out of reach. "I don't like dwelling on the past. Time to move on."

Gentle. He willed himself to be gentle. "Then, why did you tap my shoulder the other night?" he asked. And then, Henry sneered at him, lockjawed and pitifully angry. He gave the impression of a nasty little rodent baring its teeth.

Thunder. It was a sudden deafening boom that shook them all to their core, so loud and furious that Morris yelped. A second later, the patio filled with a bright whiteness that came with such force that all four fell out of their chairs, thrusting their arms in front of their faces. Then rain pummeled down. They scrambled back under the large awning of the dining area as the storm resumed its angry course. Cook came running out to meet them, oval-eyed, one hand grasping a bottle while the other waved frantically. "Oh, my Lawd! I think lightning struck Jesus!"

They all laughed as they rushed inside

The guest house was a drinking place with a Victorian problem. It was ornate and untidy, with heavy drapes and brightly cushioned furniture offset against patterned wallpaper. Framed paintings, photographs, and little displays held porcelain figurines, decorative vases, and other pretty little things. A collection of dead people's lives filled every room. As did booze; a fresh drink was always within reach.

They convened in a small glass-enclosed sunroom with wicker chairs and hanging lamps. A small heater hummed gently; the rain was steady now, beating the glass from all sides. Henry placed himself on the loveseat next to Will on the far end and was already whispering in his ear. It was a territorial move, apparent by the look in Henry's eyes, but Morris was now too tired to care. He took his seat, leaving a safe distance between himself and Jack, who was smiling eagerly at him.

"Isn't it lovely?" Jack asked, his face almost childlike as he leaned in a little close; Morris nodded and moved away.

Whiskey was poured and passed around. The storm felt romantic and dangerous, and the liquor felt necessary to survive it. One sip and Morris felt himself sink a little further.

Everyone else was alert and manic at the thought of lightning. They anxiously smoked their cigarettes and discussed the previous season's storms, talk of tornados and wind gales, that one time Flood Street lived up to its name. Even Henry was nervously prattling on. More whiskey and Morris drank to spare himself the indignity of speaking. The alcohol swirled in his gut. God, how much did these men drink? He finished his glass and found it refilled again. This was how you dealt with near-death experiences. You drank yourself safe.

"Hey, are you still with us?"

Had Morris been dosing off or merely thinking? Someone was lighting a water pipe. He took a deep hit and pushed it away from him.

A hysterical story about... a cake? A bakery?

Someone's hand was on his thigh. Then it was gone again.

A new person arrived. Towering overhead.

"Now the party can begin," someone said.

A laugh or two that turned angry.

"Is he alright?" Laughter. "Fucking tourists."

More anger, followed by a slamming door.

"What does Jesus have to do with any of this?"

"Get up, buddy. Come on. Use your legs."

He was outside and crawling into a truck. He was drifting away with the vibrating engine.

"Almost there, buddy."

Outside again. Cradled in someone's arms. Big arms, strong arms, and breath that smelled of booze and cinnamon.

"Keys. Where's his keys?"

And then a bed and an itchy feeling on his foot. *Someone's trying to peel the skin off my foot.*

He remembered the lights were on, and that hurt, until it didn't because someone had turned them off, and he was indeed alone, his arms reaching out, grasping at the air around him.

Chapter 8

Morris opened his eyes to dreary darkness. First thought: *Where am I?* He lay face down in a soggy puff cloud of fabric; he was sweating, and his head pulsed with a painful rhythm. The little clockwork gnomes in his head, the ones who usually kept the gears turning, were now chiseling deep into his skull. As his eyes adjusted to the dark, he caught the outlines of various structures: the posts of a bed, a chair rail, and the indented border of the windowpane. Finally, the pieces fell into place. He was in his hotel room.

Second thought: *I'm going to be sick.* It started as a warm sourness in his gut, but it slowly built into an aching, gnawing heat that spread throughout his veins until he was ablaze—stomach on fire with no way to extinguish it. Frantically, he threw himself to the washroom and vomited. His body convulsed and strained, and his throat burned until he expelled what felt like a whole other person. And when he could finally breathe, it started again, adding to his sense of disintegration.

Then he was sobbing, lying against the bathroom tiles. Hadn't people died from excessive vomiting? Given themselves aneurysms or torn out their throats and drowned in their blood? The sobs turned into crying, ugly crying.

One last stupid thought. He wanted his mother. Or Yasmin.

You'll survive. Yasmin's voice whispered in his ear. *People have lived through far worse.*

"It wasn't supposed to be like this," he moaned.

Sorry, my love. He imagined her there as an apparition hovering in the doorway.

"I want to go home."

Then why haven't you?

"I don't know. It's not my fault."

Yes, it is. You could have come back at any time. And if last night had worked out as you wanted, you would be perfectly happy staying where you are. What does that say about me? Yasmin's voice was now a fading afterthought; the apparition was gone.

He let out a low mournful sigh; his tainted breath lingered on his lips. "I'm sorry," he mumbled and lay there for several moments, absorbing the cold from the tiles. Abandoned by a woman who wasn't even there. It was ridiculous. Even when he played make-believe, his life was fucked up.

Eventually, he found the strength to crawl up to the sink and stared into the grotesque reflection of the mirror. He hardly recognized himself. His skin was sickly pale with bruised circles under his eyes; his hair was a stringy mess and looked thinner. Withered Morris; Zombie Morris. This couldn't be him. He said his name three times as if trying to conjure himself. Then, he drank oceans from the faucet until he replenished the lost body within him. Another look in the mirror and a bit of color had returned. Echoes of the storm reflected in his eyes, grey, the color of murky clouds. Last night, sheltered from the squall, he drank himself into oblivion because he felt empty; because he wanted to be filled up.

Eventually, he went back to bed in weak, uncertain steps and felt the mattress sink under him, but he only descended to the edge of sleep. The little digital clock cruelly blinked. It was five in the morning, and he was all alone and wanted to die.

But he did not die.

As time stretched on, the clockwork gnomes quit banging their little hammers, and the tides of nausea receded. His limbs responded to commands, his eyes refocused, and there were no apparitions or hollowness. After another horrid trip to the bathroom, the ichor was fully purged, and he drank more water, showered away the grime, and coated his face with lotion until he emerged a shade closer to his usual self. Then, he methodically packed up his belongings.

Time to go.

Online there were dozens of flights home. He wanted something early, something that would have him back in Yasmin's arms by late afternoon. Yasmin. He felt suddenly anxious to see her. Enough of their prolonged engagement, a word tossed around so carelessly for years that it practically lost all meaning. It was time to get married, time to quit chasing after every passing fancy. Maybe he should give up on the novel or at least let it rest until he had sorted his life out. It was time for a new job or graduate school, maybe both. And it was time to quit drinking as well. No more wicked binges, no more haphazard whiskey shots, and endless beer. He would never drink again, except for the occasional mimosa brunch and their Friday happy hours, but only a glass of wine or two. And he'd only smoke if he really, really wanted one. He found confidence in these little proclamations and a sense of urgency. He was so desperate to be home that he chose the earliest flight possible, forgetting his airline credit, and clicked straight through to the payment screen.

Except Morris couldn't pay.

It occurred to him that his wallet was not at hand, nor was it resting on the nightstand. He moved through the room in a befuddled manner, emptying pockets and shaking out the bed sheets, but it was nowhere. This development confused him, for he was certain he had just seen it lying out. Then, the laptop screen went dark, and a small message appeared: his session had timed out. *Dammit.* He'd have to rebook the flight.

Another ten minutes passed as he unraveled the room, searching every crevice, unpacking and repacking his suitcase. But the wallet was gone. All of his money, his credit card, his ID, it had all disappeared. How strange to think that one's entire life could be folded up so neatly, set down, and forgotten. He traced his steps back downstairs to the lobby, scanning the floors, unmindful of the desk attendant staring at him. A sickening feeling, close to panic, was starting to swell in his gut. Back in his room, he collapsed on the bed, measuring each breath. It was time to call Yasmin. But as he dug into his pocket, there was no phone to retrieve. It wasn't plugged into the charger on the desk, nor was it lying on the nightstand. It was gone. The panic grew until he was a pulsing object ready to combust. And then, he dug his head into the mound of pillows and screamed.

It took a while to calm down, to slow his breath into something manageable. *It's going to be alright,* he told himself. *Think this through.* Likely, the two objects were together, put down someplace for safekeeping. He mentally charted the course of the previous night: the bar, the Oasis patio, the little sunroom, and two separate car rides (though he could only remember the first).

One step at a time.

He used the hotel phone to dial his number, but it went straight to voicemail. Quickly, he returned to his computer and attempted to locate his phone through the app, but it was offline. Perhaps the batteries had run dry, or someone had turned it off, or… he slunk back in the chair and inhaled deeply. There was no time for another breakdown.

He surveyed the wreckage of his room. From a pair of jeans, he found a crumpled ten-dollar bill (what luck!), and there were about three dollars in loose change in his backpack. Ten cigarettes were all that was left in his crumpled pack. Thirteen dollars; ten cigarettes. One semi-clean Panama shirt and a pair of jeans. A duffel bag full of dirty clothes and an archaic laptop that begged to be put out of its misery. These were his assets.

Of course, he should email Yasmin—that was the wisest thing to do now. She would be angry, maybe furious with him, but she could still buy his plane tickets home. But then arose the questions: how would he get to the airport, and how would he pass security without a proper ID? Surely there was a DMV in town or some government office, but even then, how would he prove who he was? What an odd notion—to lose proof of one's identity and not technically exist even when you were standing there. What on earth did one do in this kind of situation?

No, it was not the right time to contact Yasmin. He knew where his things were. They were somewhere in Cook's guesthouse, of that he was certain. The more he focused, the more he could visualize them lying on the side bureau of the sunroom. They were overlooked and would still be there waiting for him. Why alert Yasmin of a problem when it is easily solvable? He would call her later from his cellphone once his tickets were purchased and he was on his way.

Back to the laptop. He typed furiously into the browser but could not find a website for The Oasis. That made sense. It was a word-of-mouth establishment that existed only for the people who needed it. It wasn't meant to be advertised. He couldn't find any information on Cook either, but then, Cook probably wasn't his real name. Even bringing up a map of the area was useless. While the town wasn't large, it was part of an intricate network of roads that spiraled outward along the surrounding hills and forests. The map held a flurry of dots, each representing unlabeled houses, and it was as daunting as searching the constellations. He had one landmark: the statue, Salvation Hill. The Oasis was in the vicinity, though he wasn't sure from what angle. Still, it was enough.

But first, food. He'd feel better once he ate. Back downstairs, he crossed into the little side parlor where a breakfast tray was waiting for him, full of stale croissants and bagels, possibly the same ones that had waited for him every day that week. He plucked up a croissant and peeled a browning banana before chugging a cup of coffee, extinguishing the remaining sparks of sickness. He was strong again. He was ready.

From behind the counter, Kenneth sat in his usual droll disposition. "I hope you're enjoying your stay," he said, though his face was angled downward into his book.

"Yes, I'm having a lovely time." Morris forced a weak smile. He wandered over to the front desk and peered over the counter. Of all things, Kenneth was reading a tattered Bible, which somehow explained why this odious little man was always so curt with him. "I was wondering, have you seen a phone down here? I might have dropped mine last night on my way in."

"No," he responded with casual indifference.

"Right. Well, you have my credit on file still, yes?" Only then did Kenneth look up at him, his brow furrowed, but at least he nodded. "Well, that's a relief," Morris said. "I might need to extend my stay a few extra days."

"We're all booked up this weekend."

Morris scoffed. The hotel was empty. The entire town was mostly empty. He opened his mouth to protest but thought better of it. There was no point in arguing. "Well, if you don't mind me asking, what day is it?"

The desk clerk glared at him. "Thursday." He said it as though he were diagnosing a disease.

Morris forced a polite smile and left the foyer, muttering *little shit* under his breath but only when he was safely outside.

At a small deli, the only one open this early, he purchased a half sandwich wrapped in cellophane, and a bottle of water, which he could refill later if necessary. Altogether six dollars and some change, which was nearly half his funds. He cautiously asked the attendant if she knew Cook or the Oasis, but she didn't. "Pity," he told her so as not to appear distressed.

Outside, he lit a cigarette. Now there were nine left. Funny how something becomes more desirable when they're in low quantity.

"Those things will kill ya!" He turned and saw an elderly man standing outside a closed antique shop. The man's bulbous stomach hung dangerously low over his belt, his beard white and patchy. Then he lit his cigarette and flashed a toothy grin.

Morris didn't stay to engage him but instead moved down Main Street toward the far end of town. The western roads split and diverged as the shops and galleries faded away. The remnants of a stone manor, perhaps once a hotel in its glory days, were now a primeval ruin covered with graffiti. He selected a road that seemed to head in the right direction and walked for what felt like a mile before stumbling upon a grocery store and a gas station. None of this was familiar.

He backtracked towards town and headed up another winding road with no sidewalk, sticking close to the grassy strip that fed into the surrounding woods. Soon he was ascending, a good sign. But then the road curved in the wrong direction, and he turned back to select another. He continued his march uphill, straddling the edge of the road, an act that saved him when a truck sped around the corner and nearly smashed into him.

Another split in the road. Morris chose to go right and eventually passed a small collective of storybook cottages. Farther up lay a small park, a level inlet with a scattering of picnic tables around a strange stone-carved shrine. A natural spring gurgled from the rock and collected in a mossy basin. It was a serene little nook that conjured the idea of pilgrims arriving and dipping ceremonial chalices in the water. No one was around; it seemed like an ideal spot to rest. He sat on one of the tables, ate his sandwich, and finished his water. Under the shade, the breeze gave a slight chill against his sweaty shirt. He smoked another cigarette, and then he had eight left.

After a suitable amount of time passed, he refocused, trying to mentally conjure the exact roads that led to the guesthouse but couldn't. He couldn't remember any details. Both rides out, he'd been drinking and distracted. He had another cigarette. And then another. How long had he been sitting here? Ten minutes? Twenty? An hour?

He had five cigarettes left in his pack, and his lungs felt clogged. He gave a weak, dry cough.

Henry suddenly came to mind with such force that he effectively blocked out all other thoughts. Poor Henry. Ugly, dirty Henry. Then, a strange thought took him. What if he was slowly morphing into Henry? He could almost feel his skin chafed and dry up, his hair turning brittle. Too much smoke and booze. He, Morris, would eventually turn into another sweaty vagabond, a man who begged for spare change. A man who sucked people off for the simple pleasure of a hot shower.

Henry knew the way to Cook's. And he was probably somewhere around town. If he found him, Henry could take him to The Oasis, by force if necessary, and then he'd get his wallet back and catch the red-eye home.

Morris headed back toward town, a much easier walk once it was downhill. It was probably noon, maybe later—stores and bars were open, and people were out, not the flood of people from the previous weekend, but enough to feel like the town's pulse was slowly reviving. He poked his head into different storefronts, quick scans for Henry or anyone else who looked familiar. Twice he stopped random pedestrians and gave them Henry's description. Then, he stopped at Tina's office, but the receptionist nervously told him she had gone out and was not expected back till the next day. Perhaps he was making a spectacle of himself, dashing around in a frenzy. People probably thought he was crazy. Best to settle down. He bought another half sandwich and refilled his water bottle with his remaining money.

It was midafternoon—at least he thought it was—not late, but not too early when he approached the Public House, the crumbling bar with its balcony and tweed couch, where his troubles had all started. In the dull afternoon light, the bar was less charming than he remembered, more of a junkman's showroom, a cluttered mess of old chrome tables and couches and the ever-present fog of smoke. To think, it had appeared magical a week ago.

A few patrons had already nested over their drinks, and though he scored a few side-eyes, they mostly ignored him.

The bartender, however, titled her head in amusement. "You look terrible."

"Yeah, well, it's been a rough week." Morris smiled wearily and peered behind him.

A small group of young people huddled at a corner table with bowed heads as if plotting secretly. Then he noticed Kenneth, that foul cur from the hotel, sitting among them and flaunting his usual scowl like the best of accessories. On the other side of the room, an elderly couple kept to themselves as they drank their cocktails in a quiet, dignified fashion. A sweaty oval-faced man with chunky glasses chain-smoked over a book. The jukebox was set to low and playing an unfamiliar pop song.

The bartender angled patiently. "You ordering or enjoying the scenery?" she asked, and Morris slid onto a stool and plucked out cigarette number five. He didn't want it, but he was restless. "Drink?"

"Well, I got about two dollars left to my name," he said. "Literally two dollars. What can I get with that?"

She inhaled her disappointment before handing him a matchbook. He lit his smoke and had four left. "Wrong day for it. Free drinks are easier to score on the weekends," she said.

"If I could trouble you for some water, please." He let his voice go low and pitiful.

"Charity case!" she called out. Morris was startled as the whole bar went silent; even the jukebox stalled. Everyone was looking up at him. The elderly man reached for his wallet, but his wife quickly slapped his hand. The bartender frowned. "Charity case!" This time with snarled force.

The reader put down his novel and waddled over. "I can do him a beer," he said, then added, "but a cheap one." A wrinkled five-dollar bill was placed on the counter, and the bartender snatched it up.

Before Morris could protest, her back was turned to him, uncapping a Budweiser. Piss water, undrinkable, but still, she placed it in front of him. "No, no. Thank you, but no..." Morris stammered. This was embarrassing.

"Go on. We've all been there before," the stranger said and moved back to his table.

"Old custom from the hippies." The bartender fished into her pack and pulled out a bundle of Marlboros. "I can spare these," she said.

He wanted to say something, but he couldn't find the words. Instead, he gave her a pathetic whimper of a smile, almost determined to let his eyes tear up.

Not one for affection, she sighed deeply. "You're welcome. I'm Amanda, by the way." This time he did thank her. "So, you want to talk about it? I got time."

"No. Not really," he said. It was all so humiliating, and he didn't have the energy to spin it. "Do you know Henry?" He described him, and she nodded. "Do you know if he'll be here tonight?"

Amanda shrugged. "Wouldn't surprise me. He's usually here throughout the weekend." Then, she departed to collect empty glasses.

Morris let the beer sit for a while before taking a sip. It brought back terrible memories and little tremors of nausea. Another sip, and he was fine, though he avoided having any more. His admission was paid, and he felt he should let it last as long as possible. Otherwise, he couldn't figure out what to do with his hands. He would cup the bottle and stroke it, rap his fingers against the worn countertop, or light a match from the matchbook and watch it extinguish. He wanted his phone. Badly.

When he built up enough courage, he turned back to Amanda. "Do you know what time Henry usually shows up?"

"Later than this. Sorry." She emptied the ashtray and replaced it with a fresh one.

For an hour, he sat there brooding. He'd never considered himself a passive person, but there he was, waiting for something—anything—to come swooping in the front door and save him. A few other people entered, but they weren't the ones he was looking for.

Amanda leaned over the bar, lit her cigarette, and examined his beer bottle, which was still half full. "Are you sure you don't want to chat? You look broken," she said.

At first, he had no idea what to tell her. "I've made

some terrible mistakes, and I don't know how to fix them," he said. It had all started somehow with Henry, both missing and hating him, his writing and wanting an affair and not wanting to leave until he actually did, and the various acts of self-sabotage that led him here: desperate and broke and powerless to do anything about it. However, there were no words to describe it all. "I lost my wallet! And my phone," he said. "I had them last night, and they're gone. They're just gone…" He began to ramble, unsteadily, about not having a plane ticket. He avoided the topic of The Oasis, though the way Amanda looked at him, she probably knew he'd been there.

"What are you going to do?" As opposed to "Are you alright?" She wasn't going to save him.

For a moment, he considered asking her about Cook. Did she know the way? Could she contact him? But he felt too ashamed to say anything. "If I can find Henry…"

"You think Henry has your stuff?" she asked.

"No. But I think he can point me in the right direction."

Amanda considered this for a moment. "I can make a few calls. No promises, but maybe I can get him for you." And then she slammed her open palm against the bar. "Charity case! This guy needs another!"

There were grumbles around the bar. Morris hadn't even finished his first beer and hadn't planned to. He began to protest, but she shushed him.

"Come on now," Amanda said. "I don't make the rules."

This time it was Kenneth who answered the call. He looked different than he did when stationed at the hotel.

Without the prim maroon uniform, he carried himself more boldly with a shady sort of pretentiousness. His black shirt made his face look pale and severe. There were dark circles under his eyes that Morris hadn't noticed. From behind, the young men laughed at the gesture as if charity were beneath them.

"I got his next one," Kenneth said and put his money on the counter.

Amanda took a guarded stance, her face creased in hard lines, but silently, she replaced his cash with another uncapped beer. As Kenneth walked away, she whispered to Morris, "Be careful around them." Then she moved to the back and out of sight.

The new beer felt cold in his hand; he drank a little more and wondered if he kept drinking, would it change a thing?

Chapter 9

Beer, beer, lots of beer, and all in the name of charity. Morris continued to fade into the softer side of inebriation, arranging his bottles around him like an amphitheater. The bottles stared at him like little friends, half consumed, all submissive and attentive listeners. Had he been muttering to himself?

The Public House was filling up, slowly at first, but then in a steady flow. Amanda quickly lost track of him. Supposedly, she'd made a few calls on his behalf, and someone would eventually come for him. Who or when she did not specify. It didn't matter; Morris was in the hands of the people now, who were plentiful and very generous. Word had gotten out that the strange little tourist sitting alone was destitute. Even as he cradled a half-full bottle, another one appeared next to him under the call of "Charity!" Best to leave it alone and save it for later. No, he didn't need another one. He still had two to finish. But maybe a cigarette? His pack was empty, and now he was being fed them one at a time. Someone had ordered him a club sandwich with chips, and poor

Amanda was forced to rush back into the kitchen to make it, leaving the other bartender to clear up tables frantically.

"So, what happened to you?" someone asked.

He was on autopilot, mechanically retelling his story, only elaborating when someone probed:

I was at the artist colony... because of the blackout, I overslept and missed my flight home... I got sick and missed my second flight... my wallet's gone... so is my phone... I have no money... I'm stuck... But I have a friend who is coming for me... maybe...

The good people ate up every word so fast they could choke. His tragedy was a feast, and they salivated over it. They bought Morris beer after beer, demanded he drink up, and patted his shoulder. Then they were lost back in the crowd, smiling to themselves for their contribution as if his problems had magically resolved the moment they stepped away.

He knew he couldn't sit there forever. Too much idling, drinking, slouching—he was starting to lose sense of himself. He abandoned his seat and moved about the bar. A white-haired man in a cowboy hat bummed him a cigarette, which he smoked in front of the entranceway. At any moment, Henry would come in looking for him, and he wanted to be ready.

Another hour passed, and he found himself face-to-face with Kenneth, who observed him with distilled apathy.

"Charity case?" Morris said glumly and received another beer to hold.

"You can sit with us if you like." And then Kenneth pointed back to his table where his friends crowded together.

This is how it starts, he thought. "No, thank you. I'm waiting for somebody," Morris replied.

"You've been waiting all day. You only get charity a few times before people lose interest," Kenneth said.

Morris hovered in place as Kenneth returned to his corner table, taking his seat among the box-cut group of unkempt boys. They looked like overgrown teenagers from a distance, the kind that stared out territorially from the back of a high school cafeteria. *Be careful around them.* He felt Amanda's warning in the back of his mind, yet he was tired of standing there, so he sullenly walked toward them. It was as if they were expecting him, the way they collectively scooted to make room for an additional chair.

"What's up, Charity Case?" This came from a swollen young man, who was only distinguishable by his red cap and weak mustache that looked more like a dirty lip.

"This is Morris Hines," Kenneth said. "Staying up at the Stoney Brook."

"Yeh? So, what happened to you?" another one asked.

"I'm sorry, but I don't want to talk about it," Morris replied. "It's been a rough couple of days."

The boys shrugged in unison and continued in their regular way. It was difficult for Morris to keep one eye on the door and follow their overlapping conversations: cheap talk about sex and sports and something about pinball kept surfacing. Were they gonna play pinball; so-and-so was a terrible pinball player. It sounded like code.

"Do you guys hang out at the arcade?" Morris finally asked.

One of the boys piped in, "Why? Are you another pinball player?"

"Stop it," Kenneth said. "He obviously doesn't get it."

The guy in the red cap leaned in close; his hot breath poured out like mist. "Hey, see that girl over there?" He pointed a chewed fingernail to the far side of the Public House. It took Morris several moments to recognize whom the man was gesturing towards. "Whatcha think?"

She was a lithe blonde girl, staring dreamily into space while her friends talked. Everything about her was aerie and light; she seemed like the kind of young woman who still slept with dolls and paraded around the house in ballet slippers. "She looks very shy," Morris said diplomatically.

The Red Cap let out a little cluck. "Yeh, she'd want you to think that." His grin widened. "We go to the tech school together. Keeps her head down, does her work, and barely talks to nobody. But a few weeks ago, I'm sitting next to her on the bus. I give her a nod, mind my own business, and then she lays her coat out over her lap. Don't think anything of it until I feel her hand digging into my pocket. At first, I was like, what the fuck? Is she trying to rob me? But that's not it. She spends the entire ride fiddling around in there, stroking me up until I almost creamed myself." The man gave a salesman's smile, all teeth and pride.

All Morris could do was nod. He did not like the direction of this conversation.

"You should give it a try. She's quiet but nasty fun."

"Well, not my type," he said and then realized it was best to play along. "Her friend, she's more my type." He pointed out the curvy brunette next to her; he could have pointed at anyone.

"Wouldn't recommend it," Red Cap gloated. "Almost got there, but her pussy stank!"

Morris shot him an offended look and downed his beer just as another one of the boys piped in. "Well, she had plenty to say about your pigly little dick."

"Jesus Christ, shut up," Kenneth said, the disdain radiating off his face. "What if Scott heard you talking like that?"

Red Cap turned sulky for a moment. "We're just talkin'."

The group fell silent Morris glanced back over his shoulder. There weren't any seats left at the bar and Amanda avoided his gaze. Finally, the silence broke when Kenneth asked him where he was from.

"Washington, DC," he replied. There was a collective awe from around the table, but no further questions. He fumbled with his bottle, remembering what Kenneth had told him. *Don't lose interest.* "It's not as fancy as it sounds. It can be kind of awful. Everyone you meet is a lawyer or a government worker. Even the baristas think they have a PhD in political science."

There were grunts of amusement and a few smiles. "So, what does that make you?"

"A slacker." There was a slur in Morris's voice; he made a mental note to annunciate better.

The group approved of this, and there was more chatter. One of them was anxious to learn more about government agencies. He obviously watched spy films and political thrillers and wanted to know all about the CIA, which Morris knew very little about. But the young man wouldn't be deterred. "You could be an agent, and we wouldn't even know it," he said.

Morris gave another hopeful look at the doorway. "I guess," he said dismissively. "Look, here's what I know. If someone tells you they work for the CIA, they're either lying, or they're an analyst or work in IT. But, if someone tells you they work for the Department of Agriculture and don't go into details… they're an agent, and they've killed people."

A slight pause followed by another round of chuckles. He had done it—he was officially a character of interest. Then, the familiar tone of "charity case" echoed, and he was rewarded with yet another beer. The sight of it made his stomach uneasy.

"So, what are you doing here?" another person asked.

"I was at the Manderlay Colony," Morris started, his mind tracing back over the last few days. Only later did he realize his mistake in mentioning it. He had opened the door and let them peek inside, and now that he had their interest, they put their feet in the doorway to prevent him from closing it up. They had questions. There was little interest in his fantasy novel, left on a back burner so long it was smoldering, but they were interested in why he was still in town. What happened? And the details came out in stages, his fateful night running into an old college friend, the blackout, and so forth. He lingered on about the night he stowed away in his old studio, amusing them with the idea that an angry mob had chased him out. He watched Kenneth's face turn severe as he mentioned his missing wallet and phone. He was trying to avoid the details.

At first, there were the nods of solidarity, as if to say he was not the first to find himself stranded, that he would not be the last, and that beer cures all. They drank and smoked and continued to probe.

"You got nobody to come get you?" asked the man in the red cap. He was oppressively large, his body like a burlap sack holding mounds of potatoes. He lit a cigarette and choked on it until his eyes practically bulged out of his head. None of his friends moved to assist him. Finally, he pounded a fist against his chest and recovered. "Seriously," he said. "You got nobody?"

"I'd rather not call my girlfriend," Morris grumbled. "She already thinks I'm an idiot. This will be the final nail in the coffin."

"No family to come get you?"

"Stop," Kenneth said. "You're embarrassing him."

"So, who are you waiting for again?" someone else asked.

"My friend. Nobody you know." The fatigue was setting in. Morris was tired of talking and answering questions. Each one felt like a weight, dragging him down into a bottomless pit of annoyance. He was anxious for another seat to open up.

"What will you do if they don't show up?"

"I have no idea," Morris snapped. "I suppose I'll start giving blow jobs for spare change until I can afford a flight home."

Red Cap curled his mouth in disgust. Morris thought of the hotel room, the safety and comfort of four walls and a bed that beckoned him. Perhaps he could leave his information with Amanda and go back there and wait. But he'd fall asleep, and even if someone knocked on his door, would he have the strength to answer it? Best to stay put. Best to keep quiet.

"Charity case," one of them said and went to collect another round.

After that, Morris hovered in an embarrassed silence. His new beer came, and he pushed it away. He gave an occasional glance towards the door but was unsure of whom to expect. Perhaps Amanda hadn't called anyone at all. Maybe she had only said that to placate him.

More time passed, and the people around him kept changing. It had started as a small group around the table but continued to expand and retract throughout the evening. He recalled a freckled brunette sitting beside him and interrogating him over his current predicament. She bought him a shot of cheap whiskey he could barely stomach, and then she was gone. He grabbed the wrong bottle and drank someone else's beer which caused a brief scene until he was forced to retell his sob story all over again. The artist colony. Missed flights. No wallet, no phone. He needed to find Henry.

"Henry, who?"

A glance around the bar and Henry still wasn't there. Morris described him lightly.

"I think I know that guy," Kenneth muttered.

Another man, grisly and sore looking, joined them, and Morris was forced to tell the story again. He might have left his wallet at the Oasis, but he wasn't sure. Henry would know.

"I think I know that place," Kenneth said.

"How the fuck would you know about it?" Red Cap asked. Then laughter, drowned out by the buzz of conversations. Someone fucked with the jukebox, and Tom Petty was mournfully wailing in the background.

"Charity case!" Another man left the table and returned with more beer. It just kept coming.

"How do you all know each other?" Morris tried asking, focusing carefully on his speech. He was feverish and sweaty. The Public House rumbled on.

"Church. School," Kenneth replied. "Everybody knows everybody here."

"Apparently not," Morris snapped, and the man snidely grinned at him as though he were acting ridiculous.

Another beer. He had asked for water but got beer instead. He hadn't touched the last one. *Damn it.*

"I don't think Henry's coming," Morris said in a long mournful tone. "What time is it? Is it late? If I could get to Cook's place. If I could get to the Oasis, I could grab my shit and leave." He was directing this not to the table but to the universe, making one final appeal.

"I know that place," Kenneth said, this time more confident.

"What the fuck were you doing there?" someone asked. It took Morris a moment to realize the question was directed at him.

"Drinking and getting stoned. I don't remember..." and his voice trailed off. He knew he sounded like a drunkard and could feel his words stupidly swish together. And he could see the looks on their faces. They were not men, but all boys, heckling, grimacing boys, all poking fun at him. No one was calling for any more charity. "I just want to go home," Morris moaned to prove a point. And then, he was an open facet, letting the details pour out of him until there was too much for anyone to drink in one sitting. He recounted his run-ins with Henry, his doomed relationship with Yasmin, and the nights at the Oasis until he had run out of things to tell them. Dozens of empty bottles were stacked in impossible pyramids, arranged in spiraling rows around the table. It was hard to believe all that liquid was inside of him.

"I can give you a ride," someone said. "You can go get your stuff."

His head snapped up in disbelief. "You would do that?"

"Sure. I'll take you." All the men were quiet.

He had barely said "thank you" before being pulled up and whisked out of the Public House. Amanda called out to him, her voice echoing in the back of his ears, but he hadn't recognized it was her until he was outside. If he could not see Amanda, did Amanda still exist? "Wait a sec..." he mumbled, but his escorts kept him moving, down the metal staircase and another towards Flood Street and the parking lot. He felt gently guided in a series of pushes, subtle enough to feel like his actions were his own. Ahead was a car, a rusted little sedan, and then he was sitting in the back.

Night had long settled in. Darkness comes quickly in October, as do wind and cold weather. The backseat was cluttered with junk: loose papers, grime-stained towels, and mashed cigarette butts. Sitting next to him was the bulbous form of Red Cap, already choking down another smoke. Others were seated up front. Only then did he realize Kenneth wasn't among them. Morris was sure that Kenneth had been walking alongside them only a moment ago, but now he was adrift among strangers.

As the car rolled on, he pressed his face against the window, staring out at the darkened town. It slipped by in a stream of lights and shabby buildings. The radio blared some rock ballad that made the seats vibrate. He pinched himself to regain focus.

"Thank you for this," he said, though no one seemed to hear him.

"Yep. We're on our way." Someone was talking, though it was hard to hear over the music. "We'll be quick." It was the driver, talking on a cell phone. A cellphone. Connection.

Morris snapped back into his senses. "Are you talking to Cook?" he asked. Red Cap shuffled uncomfortably in his seat. "Hey! If you're talking to Cook, ask if he's got my stuff!"

The man hung up. "Be cool, dude. We'll be there soon."

The music got louder. They were now out of town and driving up into the hills, surrounded by dark woods.

"Can I use your phone?" Morris asked. He wasn't sure whom he should call or if he even knew a phone number by heart anymore, but he wanted to hold the phone, to feel the security of it.

No one responded.

"Hey!" Morris said again.

"Be quiet! I'm driving."

They continued to ascend and curve around until they had gone too far. The road flattened ahead, and the forest opened into a large plateau. Two white posts of a painted arch gleamed in the headlights. They drove through, stopped in an open parking lot, and pulled up next to another lone car. The alcohol had burned out of his mind, and Morris felt dreadfully sober. "Where are we?" he asked, but no one responded.

But Morris knew precisely where they were as if he'd always known this was the intended destination. There was an open sky and moonlight, and he could see the large gray frame of the statue, the Christ with its gaping arms. It was a colossal totem, its empty stare deadlocked with the town below. Up close, it had the cheap plastic look of a child's toy, an amateur sculpture that had been propped up in a hurry, the kind that could easily collapse and crush the unsuspecting with the weight of a juggernaut.

His three escorts exited the car without a word, and from his vantage point, Morris could make out the small campfire in the distance. Ahead of him, there was a small collective huddled around the fire; behind him, the road led into darkness. He imagined jumping out of the car and sprinting away down the road. They'd never catch him in time, but then he'd be alone in the dark wilderness. And it was cold now, far too cold for him to risk getting lost. Finally, he stepped out, felt a shrill breeze cut through him, and shivered. *You are being paranoid*, he told himself. *You're in the Tunnel. Snap out of it.* Then, he approached the fire.

"Why are we here?" Morris called out.

There were seven of them altogether. Six young men, including the three who brought him, and then a pigtailed girl in an oversized sweatshirt. All of them were huddled around the dancing flames, all looking bored and severe as if they had grown tired of waiting. The last one, the oldest looking one, clean-shaven, tended the fire, poking at it with a stick, careful not to disturb the iron pot resting on top.

"All right, Scott. You gonna say a few words?" one of them said.

"You've heard it all before. No point in repeating it." He stoked the fire, causing little orange embers to sprout up and dissipate. "Water's not ready."

Blearily, uncomprehendingly, Morris turned his face to the ringleader, Scott, his face illuminated by firelight, orange and pale and slightly androgynous. The glow gave the perception of a halo, a wicked orange halo, around his head. When Scott nodded, the other men moved forward.

"Look," Morris said, holding up his palms. "I don't want any trouble. Please, I need..."

One of them punched Morris. A quick strike to his cheek sent him stumbling backward as he stared in disbelief. Yet, he felt nothing but a series of cold pinpricks across his face. The second punch hurt. It landed against his jaw, and the pain traveled inward, into every nerve in his neck and shoulder. They stepped forward, and he fell to the ground, arms flailing as he screamed. They were all laughing at him.

He rose and was shoved back down. Someone spat on him. They lurched forward when the laughter died away, faces like vultures, sadistic and hovering, dark eyes burning in the low light. "Why?" was all Morris could muster.

"Fuck you!" And then one of them, a scrawny teenager, all limbs and bones, dashed forward, swinging his delicate soft-ball fists. They did not hurt as much, but they came in a flurry, and Morris could barely deflect them.

"Okay, stop!" The girl. Her voice was shrill. "Stop it! He's had enough!"

But the attacker had gone berserk, slapping at his head until Morris lifted his leg and kicked out. The kid fell backward with a surprised yelp. He was only a child, no older than fifteen, pimpled and ugly. By the time the boy came back at him, Morris had crouched and thrust his open palm into the kid's jaw. The boy screamed and fell over as the girl started to cry. "Shut the fuck up, Tess," someone yelled, and the mob descended. It took one more punch to the gut, and Morris was huddled on all fours, vomiting an entire evening's worth of booze. "Look at that!" "He got some on your shoe!" "Damn it to hell!" The boy had regained his footing and was angrily hopping up and down. He wanted blood, a pint for each drop formed in his injured mouth. The girl sobbed, begging for someone to take her home.

At this moment, Morris realized he was going to die. These men, these strangers, they were going to kill him. They were going to beat him into an unrecognizable pulp and leave his remains to be discovered. And he didn't even know why. Mortality had always haunted him. But he associated death with old age. He had always assumed he would be old or at least older, sitting in a bed surrounded by fluffy whiteness, loved ones holding his hands. Suddenly, he wanted his mother, his placid calm mother, who would smile ever so solemnly. What was happening now was nothing like the artistic depictions in films. Wasn't there supposed to be a long parade of memories? Where was the comforting white light? He felt a deep throbbing pain in his gut and the taste of bile in his mouth. He tried to move, but his limbs went numb. And now that there was no comfortable ending, he wanted it over and done with. He was sick to death of himself. He was sick of Morris Hines and the awful situation he'd put himself in.

An impossible amount of time, minutes that carried the weight of an hour, passed before he felt the mob converge again. He was pulled to his feet, a thick arm curled around his throat, and another was gently pinning his fighting arm behind him. There was no fight left; he only wished he was a little more reluctant.

"Bring that faggot over here," Scott said. There was no joy, no malevolent grin, only a look of disgust. He was still huddled over the fire pit, where the pot of water had begun to boil. It was waiting there to greet him. The girl sobbed again. "Someone put her in the car."

Morris stared miserably at the pot. Henry's hand looked burned; the skin was twisted and malformed.

"Do you know your Bible, faggot?" Scott stared with the look of something prophetic. His arms were raised, flannel shirt flowed like an open robe. "As when the melting fire burns, the fire causes the waters to boil, to make your name known to your adversaries, that the nations may tremble at your presence."

Morris was pulled toward the bubbling water, his free arm grasped and held out before him. No point in struggling; no strength left. *Maybe it will only hurt for a moment...*

Headlights appeared from the road, and everyone froze. Morris, caught in mid-procession, turned to see the flashing lights of a siren, and then came the release; the hands that held him let go, and he fell to his knees. Two men ran off towards the woods, but the rest stood in place. The one they called Scott straightened himself up, raising his chin with pompous dignity as the police cruiser positioned itself at the tail end of the parked cars.

Morris felt his body almost sink against the cold earth. He was breathing easier now. He was going to live and wanted nothing more than to find the strength to rush forward, to knock the cauldron of water onto Scott's legs. But he didn't move. He watched the tall man exit the police cruiser, pistol drawn in one hand, flashlight arched out in the other.

"Stay where you are. Hands up!" Morris recognized the voice immediately. Atherton. "Scott Skeel! I told you last time I'd put a bullet in you if this happened again."

Scott crossed his arms. "But you won't, will you?" he said. No smile, no gloating, no challenge. It was a simple declaration. "You won't now. You won't ever."

The girl continued to sob into the baggy sleeves of her sweatshirt.

"Give me a reason," Atherton snarled. He shook his gun as if realigning it with Scott's face. "Morris, get up and walk to me. No one else moves."

How quickly men change into frightened children when a louder voice commands them. Their rage and bloodlust withered away until they were trembling little boys, all lined up and waiting for punishment. And Morris was now steady and strong enough to walk out of their reach until he leaned against the cruiser. He gave them one last look, up and down, and found none dared to return it.

Atherton moved forward, gun angled, slow, steady steps ahead. The group stepped away at his approach, all except Scott, who remained sentinel by the fire. Soon, Atherton was upon him and, in a swift movement, brought the flashlight down hard against his face, a loud crack, the light flickering in and out as the group gasped, watching Scott fall backward.

"You fucker!" Scott screamed. "I'll kill you!"

Atherton fired, and the sound ricocheted from all around them. It was unclear where the bullet landed, perhaps off in the woods or nearby ground. It didn't matter. Scott screamed, arms covering his face, legs kicking frantically, too scared to know he was unharmed. He wasn't so tough now. What was left of a prophet when the piety drained out of him in a warm puddle of piss?

"I've had enough! You boys ain't smart enough to let old deeds die, are ya? You fucking morons. Do you want this town to die? One body and no one will come. And if no one comes, it means no money. That means no hotels, no stores, no jobs, and ya'll be sitting on your fat asses, remembering the days when you could afford your meth."

Morris quit listening. The pain was all over him, a dull steady throbbing that stemmed from his jaw and ran through every thread of his body, each muscle pulsing and burning. But otherwise, his bones were intact. He was going to live. He would see the dawn and have another day to worry over.

"This town was something before the likes of you showed up," Scott spat out. He was practically crying. Atherton moved as if to stomp on him with a raised boot, and again, Scott cried out.

"Pathetic," Atherton said. He backed away, gun still drawn. "It ends tonight," he announced. "Next time, there will be retribution." This was a word they all understood in its many forms.

At the car, he pushed Morris into the passenger seat, the high beams capturing the group like paralyzed deer, all staring forward. In a swift movement, Atherton tossed his pistol into the glove compartment, and only then did Morris notice the other gun, the official one, still holstered. Atherton winked at him as he pulled out, and soon they were driving away as the little mob and their campfire receded into the darkness under the shadow of Christ.

Chapter 10

They drove through the dark and down the winding roads, around sharp curves, and under the archways of conjoined tree branches. Every few moments, Morris felt a tickle at the back of his neck. a sudden panic as he envisioned a world full of traps and pitfalls. His head would snap around, searching the road behind them for pursuing headlights. Thankfully, there was only sweet, comforting darkness, and he was safe inside, feeling the rhythmic hum of the engine trying to soothe him. Finally, he leaned against the side door and heaved a tired sigh.

"Don't fall asleep," Atherton warned.

"I couldn't if I wanted to."

His body hurt all over. His stomach was tender from where they'd kicked him. His jaw throbbed from where they punched him. What he wanted now was a hospital. He imagined being laid up in a soft bed with an IV drip and kind-faced nurses hovering over him, ensuring his parents were on their way. As the cruiser approached the long stretch of the highway, Morris finally muttered the word "doctor."

"If you can breathe and walk, you're fine," Atherton replied.

That comment bled onto him like another wound. He was not okay; he was in pain. He flashed an angry look at Atherton but then turned away. He forced a cough, hoping blood would spit out onto his hand. It didn't.

From the highway, they detoured into the parking lot of the Lighthouse Diner. It was an unextraordinary place, no better or worse than any other. They slumped into the nearest booth as a haggard-looking waiter approached, giving Morris one hard look over, and without a word, deposited two coffee cups at their table.

"Order something," Atherton said.

But Morris pushed his menu away. He was curled against the window, staring out into the parking lot. "I can't. I have no money," he said. He could not fathom the idea of food, not now. He was not hungry. The pain had simmered down into a disturbingly numb feeling, almost ghostly. Everything around him felt far away as if he were staring down upon himself, observing himself from afar, curled up like a battered orphan. He pinched the flesh of his wrist and let his fingernails grind into the skin, and he still could not feel it entirely. He kept reminding himself, *You're safe now*.

"Did they steal your money?"

He drifted back. Everything was closer now. He could sense the heat rising off Atherton's body. "They wanted to kill me. It wasn't about money."

"Nah. They weren't going to kill you. Scar you, yes, but not murder." Atherton lit a cigarette, and the waiter deposited a black plastic ashtray. "Please eat something."

Morris sat up and steadied himself, arms still folded over his tender stomach. "Why didn't you arrest them?"

"What good would it have done?"

"They should be in jail. Why didn't you do something?"

There was no angry outburst or clenched fist against the table, but something changed within Atherton. There was a darkness in him, the way his eyes narrowed, the subtle snarl of his red-red mouth. He looked ready to bite. "I *did* do something. I came as soon as Amanda called me. Now order something."

When the waiter returned, Morris reluctantly ordered fried eggs on toast, which came up on an overstuffed plate. The act of chewing hurt at first, but he was famished—he knew that now—and he couldn't fit enough into his mouth as he tried to swallow down the congealed food in large chunks. He drank the coffee, then water, and more water. Only then did he feel human again. When he was done, he went to the restroom and rinsed his face under the rusted faucet. The mirror told a terrible story: his face was like a corpse, his jaw bruised with ugly pigments of pink and purple—and it would only worsen. A patch of dried blood rested at the edge of his hairline, which now seemed thin and straggly. *I don't look like this*, he pleaded with himself. He poked at the dark puffiness that blossomed under his eyes. He wanted justice. He wanted revenge.

As he returned, Atherton watched him carefully, raking his fingers through his mutton chops in deep contemplation.

"Who was that guy tonight?" Morris asked as Atherton sucked in air through his teeth. "I want to know."

"That asshole was Scotty Skeel. He's a psychotic fucker, but then his whole family is. Half of them were eaten up in the meth trade, the other half are puritanical crazy, and you can probably tell Scotty's a bit of both."

"But why attack me?"

"I think you know why." Atherton gave him a solemn look, which made Morris balk.

"I didn't do anything."

"I'm sure you didn't."

He felt his face buckle, nerves twitching. "There has to be a reason," he muttered.

Atherton let out a low sigh. He'd given this speech before. "Look, there's still people around here who don't like change and don't like what the town's turning into. Their influence gets weaker every year, and they ain't happy 'bout it. Usually, there's peace, but sometimes, Scotty gets biblical and wants to leave his mark. Consider yourself guilty by association."

Morris felt his indignation rise. "So, if he's done this before, why haven't you arrested him?"

"It's complicated."

"Please. For my own mental health, explain it to me."

Atherton let out a sigh. He looked tired of the conversation. "Let me put it like this. The Skeels have been here for generations. They own a lot of property. I'd have Scotty rotting in a cell right now if it weren't for the fact that his daddy owns half the buildings in town. There's a balance to maintain. He keeps rents low, shops stay open, and we all deal with the occasional… outburst."

Morris leaned his head onto the dirty tabletop. "Like the Wicker Man?" He thought of Scotty and the Skeels as a multi-headed beast, something satiated with a yearly sacrifice. Such a disturbing thought: he almost had been a sacrifice.

"What? The Nic Cage movie?"

When the waiter deposited their check, Atherton paid and ran his fingers through the mass of Morris's hair in a gentle, comforting motion. The entire act was at once condescending and yet tender. It was a touch that lingered. Then, Atherton pulled three twenty-dollar bills from his wallet and laid them out on the table.

"Take this," he said. "You'll get hungry again."

Sixty dollars. Such little money, and yet it felt like a fortune. "I can't accept this," Morris said, knowing full well the offer wouldn't be revoked.

"It's a loan." Atherton turned his head away, allowing Morris the dignity of snatching it up without being watched. "Shall we head out?" he finally asked.

"Don't you want to know what happened?" Morris said. "Why I'm still here?"

"Tomorrow. We'll worry about all of it tomorrow."

They didn't go back to the hotel. It wasn't safe, Atherton claimed. Instead, they drove back through the promenade, where the pubs had finally extinguished their lights. Downtown was deserted, with only a single drunkard swaying under a lamppost. Morris sat in the patrol car, eyes glazed as he examined the abandoned streets, part of him wishing they could continue driving on forever.

Atherton stopped at the very end of town in front of a squat brick building, angled up towards a side street as if it had been tossed here in a haphazard fashion. The building held a small junk shop masquerading as an antique store on the ground floor. Morris glanced over the display window, able to see the outlines of an oversized loom half-threaded among collections of old books and painted vases and wooden mannequins. He wondered how such a broken-down disorganized store could survive among its storybook neighbors.

"Why are we here?" he asked, but Atherton didn't respond. He disappeared down the side alley, and Morris cautiously followed. The back alley opened in a long corridor of hidden apartments layered upon each other on the backends of the shops. Makeshift porches held potted plants and folding chairs among the garbage bins. People actually lived here, away from view, on the edge of squalor. *What kind of people live in a place like this?* he wondered.

His jaw ached.

Atherton ascended an open stairwell that led to the antique store's second floor and paused on the stoop. When Morris joined him, he jiggled the keys in the lock a second and then a third time, perhaps a little ritual, and the door slid open.

The upstairs apartment was full of junk, layers upon layers, overflowing from the antique store below. A glass bureau held tchotchkes, while a claw-foot secretary and bookshelves were arranged to create little passageways. There was stuff everywhere: vases and floor lamps, stacks of old magazines, and framed landscape paintings covered the walls in a perturbing mural. A light scent of mold gave the sensation of a damp fog hovering over a cave, a bandit's lair full of stolen treasures.

There, standing among the wreckage, was Henry. Elusive Henry with the hobbit cheeks and the tangled hair pulled back into a drooping ponytail. Chubby Henry, wearing his long nightshirt that puffed out over his belly.

It wasn't easy to interpret the look on Henry's face. It was at once bored and disturbed, his mouth slightly curved into a frown as he stared forward, studying him, accessing the damage. All Morris could do was stare back. And there was Atherton, eating up their discomfort.

"Come on now. Say hello to your friend," he instructed.

Henry looked stunned. "You look l-like shit," he stammered.

"I'll set up a bed for you," Atherton said and moved to the back end of the apartment where the junk piles hollowed out into a small sleeping alcove: a twin bed and a nightstand surrounded by dressers and stacked boxes and duffel bags. A little stand held a TV. It all created the illusion of a bedroom, though there were no formal walls. Atherton unfolded a small military cot and laid it out, and now the nook slept two.

On the opposite wall, an archway led to a decrepit kitchenette, shabby and rust stained with the dank smell rising from the sink. Then, there was the little washroom so cramped that one could shit and shower all at once.

"No hot water," Atherton warned. "Henry usually goes up to The Oasis to bathe."

This caught Morris's attention. "How do you get there from here? Is it far?"

Atherton let out a soft chuckle. "I'm sure if you're nice to him, Henry can show you the way. Anyway, it's getting late. Make yourself at home."

"But my stuff! It's still at the hotel."

"Tomorrow," Atherton said with a flick of his wrist. He was already wading back out towards the door. "Everything will get figured out tomorrow."

And then, they were alone for the first time in years, and neither of them knew what to do. They shuffled in place without speaking. Around them, various objects seemed to shift without actually moving; an odd creak in the floorboard lurched as one of them moved their foot. They inhabited their silence and gave nothing away.

"Why are you here?" Henry finally asked.

Morris shot him a tortured look, unable to comprehend the question. The fatigue was setting in; all he wanted was to lie down.

"Why are you *here?*" Henry asked again, this time with accusation.

"Not by choice." Why was he asking this? *I was attacked. I almost died. Why are you talking to me like this?*

Henry flung his arm out in a lyrical, discus-throwing swipe and pointed a gnarled finger at him. "You were supposed to leave!" Such anger, enough to make the tower shake, to come crumbling down, brick by brick. "Why are you here?" Henry screamed.

The door flung open. Atherton came half lumbering, half gliding toward them. His hand rose and slapped Henry across the face. Hard. A quick, brutal movement that sent Henry toppling over a stray box. Even Morris jumped at the suddenness of it. The adrenaline surged and brought those dueling instincts of flight and fight, but he felt frozen in place.

"We've talked about this," Atherton said in a low growl. "What did I tell you about raising your voice here?"

Below him, Henry whimpered. His body curled up, bracing for another strike.

"Come on. What did we talk about?" The tall man's foot gently nudged him. There was the smallest trace of patience in his voice—a thin, frail patience pulled tightly enough that it could snap with the slightest amount of pressure.

What was Henry now when his fiery pistol was out of ammo? He was now defenseless, broken, all the fight in him extinguished. Even as he rose, his body trembled, tears budding in his eyes as he rubbed his cheek. Age had melted off of him, leaving the visage of a frightened child ready to break out into ugly sobs.

"Knock it off," Atherton grunted, fists tightening.

"That's enough," Morris said. His heart stopped, and his face went pale as Atherton turned toward him. "Please… it's enough," he whispered, and then he braced himself to be slapped as well.

But Atherton's face relaxed, almost willing itself calm. "Right. It's enough," he muttered. "Now, Morris, most neighbors don't know I keep lodgings here. Maybe a few, but city ordinances being what they are, it's no good advertising you're up here. All it takes is one complaint from the right asshole, and I get slapped with a few fines, and people like poor Henry have no place to sleep."

"Understood," Morris said without hesitation. He slowly unclenched. "Thank you, sir."

Atherton raised an eyebrow at that last remark but ultimately approved. Henry still stood there, buckling his mouth as he rubbed his cheek, his eyes now large and swollen into the loud orbs that lecherous Japanese cartoonists had built entire religions around. At any moment, streams of tears could come flowing out from them.

"It's all right now," Atherton said, using his gentle voice. He reached out and cupped Henry's shoulders. "I know this is stressful for you." He pulled Henry in and embraced him like a father hugging his traumatized son. "There's my boy," he said. He then tucked Henry's head under his chin, a thick hand grazing along Henry's spine. "My poor sweet boy. You'll be good now."

Without another word, Atherton left, letting the apartment door ease shut behind him.

Alone again, and the tension began to unravel. It became easier to breathe; only as his heartbeat slowed did Morris realize it had been pounding furiously. Henry also looked deflated. He collapsed onto his bed, burying his face into the mounds of pillows, waxing and waning with each breath. Morris watched him, first in horror, then disgust, but finally with a pang of affection. At least they were together now.

"Does he do that often?" Morris finally asked.

"No." Henry's voice was muffled in pillows. "It's rare."

"It's still not right."

"I guess." There was a stony resilience in Henry's voice. He was up from the bed with newfound composure, the arrogance gone and replaced with stoicism. His face was like granite, hard-edged with cracks, but still dignified. "You met the Skeels tonight, didn't you?"

The Skeels. The scene played out in Morris's head through a kaleidoscope of grainy images. "Yes," he replied. It all seemed as intangible as the constellations, what should only happen to other people in far-off places.

They idled around each other for a moment until Henry got up and turned on the small television set. Such an antique thing. It was a shock that it worked. Underneath the static, a talk show with canned laughter.

"You got any money?" Henry asked.

"A little. Atherton gave me some."

"Well, don't spend it. That's how it starts. Before you know it, you're in his debt." He was nesting again on his bed, getting cozy. "Tomorrow, call Yasmin or your parents and get out of here."

"I need to get back to the Oasis first. Can you take me?"

Henry flipped through channels until he settled on a reality show, beautiful people with beautiful, funny problems. "Atherton will take you."

"Phone?"

"Downstairs in the shop."

Morris suddenly felt a chill, a clutching, grasping, menacing chill. He was now scared of the dark and all it could harbor. The thought of the antique store below brought images of dark figures, all waiting for him, all chanting and evil, all ready to harm him. He didn't dare venture out now. At least here, there was plenty of light and a locked door.

As for Henry, he had already drifted away. He was in bed, bundling himself up in the same methodical way a cat circles its bedding before it lays down.

With nothing left to say, Morris made his way to the little washroom with hopes of a shower. One look, however, and he decided against it. The little stall was filthy. Patches of mold collected in the corners; the cake of soap was worn down with threads of hair embedded in it. Disgusted, he turned away, wishing for the comfort of the hotel. Henry had left a single lamp on, and with the glow of the TV, shadows danced in the dark corners of the attic apartment. He got a drink of water from the kitchenette faucet and rummaged around for a pack of cigarettes before finally giving up. The night weighed heavily as he peeled off his rank clothes, wincing as he did it. Then he was lying in his cot.

He thought of violence, sadistic violence. It came down on him from all sides. The weight of it fell over him until it was almost impossible to move. *I almost died*, he said to himself in grim repetition. The world outside was terrifying, and he was trapped with someone who hated him. He thought of the sanctity of home, his plush bed, and how violence never found him there. *I want to go home.* Knees bent up, back curved, guarding his underbelly against unseen assailants. *Home.* He was trapped here now.

This was home.

Eventually, he slept.

Chapter 11

Henry's mind was laid out as a narrow hall of mirrors. Mirrored walls, mirrored floors, a mirrored door at the end that opened to an identical passage where his image reflected from all sides. As such, he saw himself in the most random of details. The sight of pressed table linens made him tug at his wrinkled clothes; the sound of windchimes had him consciously aware of his tone of voice. The scent of smoke and the taste of burnt toast, and he instinctively placed his scarred hand in his pocket. Sometimes, he would wander downtown in a daze, lost in his thoughts, and his gaze would fall upon the nearest windowpane. Among the storefront displays, his ghostly image would appear in the glass. He always found himself drawn to his reflection, inspecting the contour of his face with a sense of bewilderment and thinking, *what the hell happened?* He had been a boy for so long that he did not know how to be anything else. And yet, it was always a grown man staring back at him.

It was not out of vanity that he did these things, though he'd been quite vain when he was younger.

It was an act of self-monitoring. The past existed outside the hall of mirrors, a vast archive of failures and disappointments. It was full of self-pity, embarrassing at parts, and unchangeable. Henry was happier in the moment, focusing on the present wants and needs he could control.

Only when he felt particularly masochistic would his mind wander past the hall of mirrors. He would be alone in the squalor of the attic apartment and suddenly find himself envisioning his childhood bedroom. It was a painful memory, a broken bone that never properly set and required a little massaging from time to time. His old bedroom was perfect; no room could ever live up to its standards: rich wood trim against the plush carpet, the glow-in-the-dark stars covering the ceiling, the picturesque window overlooking the woods. He had decorated the walls with murals of magazine cutouts and movie posters; there was his overstuffed bookshelf, his ornate writing desk, and the hoard of action figures he refused to outgrow, all standing ever vigilant from their various perches. He could still picture himself there, a lithe teenager, lounging on his bed, listening to music, masturbating, snuggling his stuffed lion, Pimba. Oh, his lion—after all these years, he still longed for Pimba, to stroke him, to cuddle him, to sleep against his mane. And where was he now? Probably in storage, crammed in some box at the back of his parents' garage, waiting to be rescued. One day, he would go back and retrieve him.

But that was no longer possible. That bridge was long burned, all the way down to the cornerstones.

Of course, the thought of his childhood bedroom was the gateway to his family: his earnest father, his bubbly mother, and the herd of older siblings, all equally loud and competitive. They were the reason why his bedroom was a sanctuary. He often hid from them because he was often at war with them and harbored a little devil inside of him, one that craved chaos, one whose ambrosia was his family's wrath. Wasn't that the role of the youngest child—to create havoc without even trying? It was a reputation that followed him even long after those impulses began to fade.

He wrote them a letter once. It was a short note, drunkenly scribbled on a page of fancy stationery from the store. Though he left the details vague, he had carefully spelled out where he was and how he could be contacted. For weeks, he achingly waited for a response, but none came. Each week, his expectations dropped until the memory of the letter itself faded, and it was easy to rebury them all again.

Other parts of his past were less easy to ignore. Memories came in waves, each one more cringe-worthy than the last, threatening to crash against him, to knock him off his footing, until he was drowning in them. He had been a grifter, a drunk, a vagabond. He left DC behind for an impoverished summer in New York before a year-long residency in Philadelphia and slowly continued along the Amtrak corridor. He consumed friends and lovers with the same voracity he consumed cigarettes, sucking them down to the filter before reaching for a fresh pack. It took years to exorcise that little devil inside him, yet it was always there, dormant, sniffing out new conflicts.

Looking back, he could see his missteps; he was aware he had earned his reputation. But there were other sides to him, as well. He was competent and resourceful. When he found work, he dove in headfirst until he mastered whatever crafts he needed. Traits people often forget: he was generous with his money and very intelligent. He was well-read, intuitive, and an ideal companion for the museum and theater. People quickly forgot he was a force of personality, had the gift of gab, the harbinger of gossip. That was what he wanted most. He wanted to be a person of consequence, a valued opinion, and the topic of conversation long after he left the room. He wanted to be mysterious.

Once, he told an ex-lover, "Look, I can't have you knowing all my secrets."

"Secrets?" The man gasped. "What secrets? You never shut up!"

This was why Henry was always on the move. With each new residence, his past was buried, and he alone could choose what parts to excavate.

Five years ago, he'd come to town hoping to be a mysterious stranger again. His companions were two middle-aged men, a jolly couple from Richmond on the verge of retirement, who had great plans of opening a little guesthouse in the country. They painted a picture of a storybook inn where wine was poured generously, tubs filled with rose water, and a garden close to godliness, where work and play melded together like the filling of a pie. It was a pleasant portrait, one Henry at first struggled to see himself in, but as his life in Richmond had not taken shape, on the morning of their departure, Henry was there, his bags packed, ready to join them.

The town was more than they imagined, something plucked from the glossy pages of a travel magazine with its stone walkways and pastel buildings, the fairy grottos with their stone emblems. Henry was optimistically cautious. There was an oppressive friendliness that he could not deny was appealing. Their first night at dinner, strangers hovered over their table with warm welcomes. Free drinks were easy to score at the Public House, and he could swim for free at the Oasis if he paid attention to the right person.

The inn was in poor condition, but it was well placed among the Victorian Gingerbreads and a short walk from the fabled Manderlay Colony. Construction began immediately, working alongside a handyman to strip wallpaper and wood rot and replace floorboards and cupboards. It was weeks of toil, of cold showers, cooking over a camping stove, and sleeping together in the one habitable room. But there was pride in that work, that slow building excitement of seeing spaces transform. Henry left his mark on the main parlor, selecting the velvet chaise lounge with the medallion wallpaper, and stocking a bar with rescued cordial glasses. Money was easy to spend when it wasn't his; he commanded the handymen to re-sand the floor and add the crown molding, even when it no longer matched the other rooms. Upon the parlor's completion, Henry looked over it with a sense of pride and began envisioning a future here, serving guests trays of aperitifs while they chatted. As the restoration continued, he became more and more confident that the inn was a permanent part of his life and that one day, when the owners officially retired, it would naturally be passed on to him.

None of this happened. For months, they worked and planned and tore apart rooms so they could recreate them. Costs spiraled as finances drizzled through a sieve until the day came when his friends, now tired of the endless project, announced they were selling the property. To Henry, the suddenness of this development felt like walking through a pane of glass. It cut deep, but it still took several moments to realize he was bleeding. Worse, Henry had not been consulted over the sale. He was simply informed that the great plans were over and they were returning to Richmond. It was the worst kind of betrayal: to be fed a dream, to change for that dream, and then to have it snuffed out without hesitation. He told them so. He told anyone who would listen. He spent two whiskey-fueled weeks around town, absorbed with his new friends, plotting maniacally on how to claim the inn for his own. And when he finally returned, he found the doors sealed shut; his friends had left without him.

This was the past. If he could rewrite it, he would start from the beginning until the ink well ran dry and he had crafted a beautiful life for himself, something full of white picket fences and friendly faces and a simple office with a desk. He'd make something stable, something reliable, where the messes were always someone else's to clean up and where the future wasn't so intangible but something to look forward to.

*

Morning crept in softly and pulled with gentle tugs. Henry awoke, sniffing the dusty air as the mattress creaked underneath him. It was early still, early enough to hear footsteps echo on the streets. After a lifetime of late nights, he now appreciated mornings when time was solely his. Except, he was not alone.

Instantly, the morning turned bittersweet. Bitter to have the past creep in as an uninvited guest. Sweet, to have the monotony of his life disrupted. Across the nook, Morris slept, coiled under the thin sheet, face swollen and discolored like the battered son of Frankenstein's monster. *Battle scars*, Henry mused. Morris was lucky—he'd waded through life for so long without any.

Strange to think that less than a week ago, he first spied Morris in the Public House, untarnished and pure, and immediately thought he was there to rescue him.

He didn't want to dwell on it.

Quietly, Henry rose and moved through his usual route of cigarette to toilet to kitchen, careful to keep his steps light out of fear of waking his visitor. There was no coffee left in the tin. Instead, he settled for bread and butter, chewing slowly, trying not to let his mind wander. But the quiet was interrupted as Morris began to groan, gently at first, mournfully, like the soughing of distant branches, but then louder and louder.

I wish he wouldn't do that, Henry thought.

A sudden cry erupted from the bed nook, and the whole attic rang with it as Henry's stomach sank. This was his penance. Morris sat upright, guarding his stomach, eyes flickering like a frightened rabbit.

With hesitation, Henry called out to him.

At first, Morris seemed incapable of speaking, inhaling his own words in muffled sobs where he might have chewed and choked upon them. "I had a nightmare," he finally spat out, whimpering in place.

Henry felt a cruel chuckle coming on; what kind of grown man needed comforting after a bad dream? Perhaps he should cup Morris's face to his chest, stroke his hair, and mother him. *Isn't that what all men want in times of crisis... their mother?* And yet, he couldn't ignore the horrors of the previous night. Morris was probably traumatized. He'd be whimpering all day without a bit of comfort. Begrudgingly, Henry went to the edge of the cot.

"You're all right. You're safe," he said.

"I dreamt they were chasing me." Morris's voice wavered. "It felt so real."

"I'm sure it did," Henry said flatly.

"I could see the church."

Henry frowned. *What church?* It was hard to tell if Morris was alert or still half-asleep. He was already rambling, mournfully describing the brick church his grandmother took him to when he was a child. He described the stained-glass windows, the stations of the cross, the ugly purple floor runners, and the harsh wooden pews. He spoke with the gravity of a stage actor, a slow, measured speech intended for an audience until Henry motioned his hand in little circles for him to hurry up.

"There were two boys I used to see every summer," Morris said. "We would sit up on the balcony together where the organ was and talk throughout the services. And then, afterward, we would go to the woods. They weren't nice boys, I knew that, but they were my friends. We would go out into the woods, throw pinecones, and break bottles and stuff. One time, we went very far out and found this little cabin. Someone was obviously staying there. There was camping gear and a crate of beer bottles, and a little fire pit. No one was around, so we trashed it. Lord knows why, but we tore the place apart. By the end, we were smashing the windows..."

"Wait. I don't get it. You found a house in the middle of the woods, and you just broke into it?"

"It was a shack. Somebody was squatting it. I don't remember. It was so long ago."

Henry sighed. As much as he wanted to extradite himself from the conversation, he felt tethered to it. It had been so long since he had paused long enough to listen to someone else's story. "Go on," he said.

"I didn't want to be there. I wasn't that kind of kid, and I even started crying because I knew we were going to get caught. We'd get in trouble or worse."

"And then?"

"And then they turned on me. I even knew it was going to happen. They went feral and turned vicious, and soon they were beating on me. One of them found a pocketknife and was waving it around and talking about how he could cut me up and no one would know. I ran all the back to my grandmother's house with them chasing me the entire way. I've never been so terrified in my entire life." Morris shifted in his bed, inching forward as if reaching for comfort. They were quiet for several moments.

"Why are you telling me this?" Henry finally asked.

"Because that's who I was dreaming of."

Henry leaned back and shook his head. None of this was true; if it was, it certainly was not what Morris dreamt about. He felt it deeply. His own scars began to itch. But he understood well that some stories were easier to tell than others; thankfully, this one was short.

"Well, you're safe now," he said drolly.

And then, Morris groaned again, letting the last bit of exhaust out, as Henry fought that mindless instinct to comfort. He allowed one quick pet on the arm, feeling the clammy texture of night sweats, before he was up, stripping off his clothes and running a bar of deodorant along his armpits. He put on fresh underwear, shorts, and a wrinkled shirt, while he felt the heat of Morris watching him dress. He found it grotesquely intimate and unnerving. Morris unnerved him. All he wanted was to get away.

"Those men from last night," Morris said. "Will they come looking for me?"

"No," Henry said with certainty.

"But what if I see them?"

"As long as you're not stupid enough to get in their car, you'll be fine." Henry was dressed and made another trip to the washroom. He threw cold water over his face and rubbed a brittle toothbrush over his teeth. He needed to get downstairs; the shop should be open soon.

Atherton would eventually come. Dark windows closed shutters. These were the things that enflamed a temper.

"Where are you going?" Again, Morris was asking questions.

"I gotta go to work. You need to wait until Atherton comes."

"I don't trust Atherton."

"And you shouldn't. Just remember what I said last night. And keep it to yourself." He watched in amusement as Morris nodded, the same dim-witted stare on his face as if it were permanently carved into him.

But there was a depth in Morris's eyes, slowly brewing, contemplating. Even without talking, Henry could sense an entire unspoken conversation between them. He could feel the questions Morris would ask about their previous life and why he'd left, and the answers were simple. Young men feel things differently, and they are prone to blame and hate, and Henry had been so young, not just in age but at heart, and was so good at spinning stories he actually believed them. All he needed was a reason for Morris to ask, and he was ready to tell.

Poor Morris. Always caught off guard. "Can you take me to the Oasis?" he finally asked.

Henry sighed. Deeply. "Another time," he said. "I have to go."

"But my wallet. It's got to be there."

"Look, Atherton can take you." He was getting impatient. "Just call home the first chance you get. Call your parents or Yasmin. Just don't get stuck here." He left hastily before Morris could respond.

People got stuck here. It wasn't often, but he'd witnessed it enough to know he wasn't the exception. Usually, they started as tourists, pale-skinned middle-management types who jumped from one existential crisis to the next. Their fetish: a simpler way of life. How quickly they parted with money that took a lifetime to earn. Sometimes, they bought into struggling businesses, renovated little cottages, or squatted in the hotels for too long until they were a permanent fixture. He'd seen them here and there, carrying food trays, slumped over a register. This was their new simpler life.

As for Henry, he spent his days managing Atherton's shop.

Unlike the attic apartment, the antique store was clean and orderly and held only the most beautiful things: neatly arranged leatherback books and collections of painted goblets, porcelain figurines, candelabras, and theater props. Throughout the summer, a steady stream of customers was always looking for a new treasure. But now, as off-season took hold, there were only a few fleeting weekends left before the long droll of winter.

The first catch of the day: a middle-aged couple entered. Well-dressed, preoccupied with their phones, and no children—the telltale sign of money. He shadowed them as they perused vintage plates and serving trays, the wife tracing her fingers along them in silent debate. They probably owned plenty of ornate things and could tell you long, exaggerated stories of how they were acquired. The husband purchased a whiskey decanter with silver trim, one of the items for which Henry had already fiddled with the price tag. He charged them sixty dollars though it was originally listed for forty. "It's German," he said. It was the kind of lie customers liked to hear. "It's very rare. And I have matching rocks glasses right here." They were very impressed and bought four glasses at the standard price. When they left, he logged the sale in an oversized binder, adjusted the numbers, and pocketed the extra.

Henry had a gift for stealing, for fiddling, for sleight of hand. When he first started in the shop, he shied away from such instincts. Getting caught would be irreparable damage. You did not cross Atherton, the man of many moods, of volatile kindness, without consequences. Still, Atherton had his blind spots. When it was clear he had little head for business and was oblivious to details, it was easy to tinker with a price tag. And as long as people paid in cash, which they often did, there was little chance of getting caught.

Henry did other things for money, things he wasn't proud of. But those things had nothing to do with the store.

Around noon, Atherton made his usual appearance, bearing his usual gifts of a wrapped sandwich and a cup of coffee. "And a special treat," he said, placing a carton of Parliaments on the counter. The expression on his face was unguessable. He wore the face of a badger, all sharp teeth and sneer under his mutton chops. "You well this morning? You sleep fine?"

Henry replied with a faint shrug. He used to love the tenderness after the storm. "Already made a sale," he said and motioned to the logbook.

"Not my favorite bottle, was it?"

"Sorry."

Atherton frowned. "Pity. I thought I might take it home at the end of the season." He wandered around the shop in the way a man wanders in and out of a daydream, half sleepwalking, half analyzing his surroundings. He adjusted a duo of ceramic ducks so they both stared out from their perch in unison; he ran his finger over a stack of books, checking for dust. "About last night..." he finally said.

Henry mumbled, "There's nothing to talk about."

"Of course, there is. I've never seen you so upset. It concerned me."

Henry fingered the folded bills in his pocket. "What did you expect?" He struggled to keep his tone soft. He didn't feel like sassing him. Not now.

"I didn't expect you to have a little freakout. You sounded deranged." Atherton grinned.

"I was embarrassed. Of all people, I didn't need him seeing me like that."

"Heh. He's in no position to judge." Atherton continued to poke through the various shelves; greedy eyes flickered over the wares. "Come on. Whatcha talk about?"

"Nothing. We weren't in a talking mood."

Another taunting smirk lit up on Atherton's face before he quelled it. "Really? Nothing else happened?"

"I think he's traumatized. He needs to go home, obviously. He's fragile, always has been. He'll break down pretty easily, and I don't need to be involved with that."

"Unlike you. Tough boy." The grinning flickered and stopped and was replaced with a solemn look. "I worry about you spending too much time alone. I thought maybe ya'all would reconcile or something."

Again, they were silent.

"Are you thinking of replacing me?" Henry asked, and Atherton turned with a sudden frustrated affection, looking as if the question deeply wounded him. "Because you can't keep him. He's got a fiancé and a job. People will come looking for him."

"Don't talk like that," Atherton said.

Henry flinched, even if it wasn't necessary. He half expected, half hoped another open palm would come crashing down on him and knock him off his stool. But instead, he felt that oppressive body, more bear than man, lean against him and envelop him in a bulking arm. The other hand gently stroked his hair.

"My poor boy. I rescued you. I kept you safe," Atherton said. "No one could replace you. You'll always be my favorite boy. And I'll always be here for you… ya know that, right?"

It was possible to love only parts of a man while hating the rest. This was Henry's favorite part, the part he would miss. Instinctively, his arms curled around Atherton's waist as he buried his head into his chest. If he could sink inside, he would have, if only for a moment. And then, once released, he was glad to see Atherton go.

Chapter 12

The attic apartment was drenched in a musty unused smell, a mixture of cardboard and wood shavings with the slightest hint of wood rot. Morris wandered around in a daze as he tried in vain to remember the previous night. How strange that he couldn't. He knew what had happened and could recite the chain of events that led to the assault, but as hard as he tried, he could not visualize any of it.

He once read an article about a car crash survivor who, despite being pinned under a vehicle for hours, could not remember the details of the accident or rescue. Dissociative amnesia, the article called it. Morris wondered if he was suffering from that now. Images of the previous night came in brief flashes and disappeared like a passing billboard on the highway. He pressed a finger against his jaw until dull pain spread out over his face and neck. But when the finger lifted, the pain instantly vanished.

In the washroom, he doused his face in cold water and inspected himself in the mirror. His jaw glowed with shades of purple and black that turned green along the edges; the bruising had spread to his cheek. If he had his phone, he would have taken a picture. Such a grotesque image, the kind of damaged face he'd seen in the crime reports in the newspaper back home. Oh, the newspaper. Another thing he'd worry about later.

At least they'll believe me. He stared into his battered reflection. *At least they'll know something terrible really did happen.*

With nothing else to do, he returned to the wreckage of the bed nook. Then, the waiting commenced into drawn-out minutes that stretched endlessly. *We'll get you sorted out tomorrow.* He faintly recalled Atherton's words and clung to them. Except Atherton was his own sort of villain: a deceiver, a corrupter, a brute. What if he had no intention of helping him? Where there should have been solid ground to stand on, doubt made the foundation crumble. Rock turned to sand, and sand gave way to water, and the water drained into a dark pit. As Morris sunk into it, he felt like he was drowning.

These feelings abruptly vanished when the attic door opened. Atherton entered, dressed in his proud uniform. He brought gifts: a wrapped sandwich and a pack of smokes. "I thought you might be hungry," he said.

Morris was and ate frantically. It was suddenly so difficult to remember the many ways he should be angry with him.

"How are you holding up?"

"I'm ugly, but I'll live," Morris replied and watched a cocky smile grow over the tall man's face. He felt a pang of affection for it. "So, what do we do now?"

"I think it's time to get you sorted," Atherton said.

*

Friday. The town was alive again, the streets filled with nomadic tourists. Eaters and drinkers were everywhere, and the smell of food washed over the streets, from the hotels down to the River Walk. A white-haired man in a woven vest strummed a guitar with his open case, collecting spare coins. The bookseller arranged hardbacks on the street side kiosk. Children ran while holding balloons on strings while toy dogs barked from their owner's purses.

They drove to the Stoney Brook and found its grand foyer full of people, bright impatient people waiting to check-in. Morris found his duffel bag and backpack neatly placed against a small claw-foot table. Luckily, no one had wandered off with them.

A surge of nervous energy eclipsed the relief of reclaiming his bags. There, behind the registration counter, was Kenneth, stone-faced Kenneth, who handed out keys as if it pained him to do so. It only now occurred to Morris that he would see him again. A white-hot fire built up in his stomach, and it quickly spread through his limbs and down into his now clenched fists. He wanted nothing more than to run forward and grab Kenneth's throat and squeeze.

"Easy now," Atherton whispered in his ear.

This did not extinguish the fire, but it subdued it enough to think rationally. After all, Kenneth had not been at Salvation Hill that night. There was no way to prove his role in the attack, even if they all knew it.

He found himself walking forward, past the line of guests, feeling Atherton's stalwart presence following close behind. And the good people parted like the Dead Sea until Morris stood at the precipice of the counter's edge.

"I guess you weren't expecting to see me again," Morris said.

Kenneth's expression was as stoic as molded clay. "Check-out time was an hour ago, Mr. Hines."

"Fuck you," he spat out. Someone behind him balked.

Cracks began to show on Kenneth's face. His eyes nervously darted from Morris to Atherton, and he hurriedly processed the bill and placed it on the counter. "Keys?" he finally asked.

Morris threw them in his face, hoping they would slice out an eye, but they didn't. Some raised their voice, but Atherton hushed them. "If I see you again, I'll kill you."

"Did everyone hear that?" Kenneth called out to the masses.

Only Atherton answered. "Nope." He placed a thick hand on Morris's shoulder and gently steered him away. "Get your things," he said. "Rest of you all, have a nice day."

Again, Morris felt spirited away, even as he stared back at Kenneth, imagining all the torturous ways for him to die. The fire was still burning, unsatisfied, and it ached him. But then, his bags were in hand, and he was guided out through the door. One last look back: Kenneth stared forward and made a sign of the cross.

Go with God.
Die in a fire.

Outside, he kept walking. A quick turn and he was in the park, circling the periphery of the central fountain with its bathing maidens, uncontrollably muttering, hit by a frenzy of emotions. He felt them all: anxiety, fury, relief, regret. They blended together into an amorphous blob, and he was trapped inside them. People were staring, he was sure of this, thinking he was a crazy person, some mind-numbed lunatic, but he did not care. He wanted to feel that swell of anger, that fire, linger in it until he was charred. Eventually, the flames died down to embers, and he slumped onto a park bench, inhaling a cigarette. Only then did Atherton approach him.

"You better now?"

"I have the urge to destroy something," Morris said.

Atherton laughed. "I like this side of you."

"If I ever see that bastard again..."

"You won't," Atherton said. "And if you do, you be smart about it. Those boys are like rats. There's never just one of them."

One sees things, the little details when the veneer is lifted. Cracks in the sidewalk that made every third person stumble; store awnings stained with rust; hardened dog turds, stubs of cigarette butts, plastic bags that danced in the breeze; the way people greeted each other and seconds later scowled as they moved away. Once Morris noticed them, they were all he could see.

They drove to the Oasis, through the hills and the labyrinthine roads. This time, Morris could anticipate, almost predict, each turn. He knew the way and recognized each landmark cottage and the archway of branches. The compound appeared in front of him as if he had willed it into existence.

The patio was empty, thank goodness. The pool was enclosed by a long foam covering; several of the umbrella stands were already disassembled. The light tunes of pop music came from the speaker as Cook danced in place while watering his ferns and the velvet cloak smoke tree. In the distance, Jack raked the first round of fallen leaves.

Cook looked up at them with delight but shifted to sudden horror. "Your face! Dear God, what happened to your lovely face?" Morris instinctively flinched as Cook reached out to him.

"Please, I don't want to talk about it."

"Show me your hands," Cook demanded. Morris's arms were still pale and freckled and otherwise unmarred. "Well, good. It could have been much worse." Even Jack stared miserably, rubbing his own fleshy jaw as if it ached in solidarity. "What can I get you?" Cook asked. "Beer? Ice?"

"No, thank you. I think I left my wallet and phone here the other night. Please, tell me you have them."

Cook glanced back at Jack, who shrugged. They hadn't seen them, but they would look. In fact, they were all welcome to look as much as needed.

For over half an hour, the four of them scoured the property, combing through the patio and under the pavilion, each one double-checking the other's work before they moved into the guesthouse. Morris stalked the sunroom, pulling back cushions and feeling through the overlapping rugs. *If it was a snake, it would have bitten me*, he kept telling himself. He could sense he was close, that they were just out of sight. But the more time went by, the more hopeless he felt. They were gone. Everything. His cash, his credit cards, his phone.

"I'm sorry, Dearheart. I wish I knew what to tell you," Cook said. He uncapped a beer and tried to get Morris to accept it.

"No. I think I've given up drinking for a while," Morris said weakly. He was suddenly back in the sunroom, moving furniture around and then inspecting the bathrooms, any crevice they could have fallen into. How many times had he done this at home, disrupting his apartment to locate his keys that were in plain sight the entire time?

"Why don't you just sit down for a second?" Atherton said.

He had the urge to snap at him, to whine and moan. He didn't want to sit. But he did as he was told and looked over the disrupted sunroom. "I promise I'll put everything back," he said to Cook, who did not seem worried.

They returned to the patio, where Atherton drank from a bottle. "You'll be alright, you know. People had lost wallets long before you and survived."

But it feels like the end of the world right now.

"So, guess this means you're staying a little longer?" Jack asked in a sheepish voice. "I got a spare room. If you need it." Morris stared at him miserably. He tried not to see the dopey hopeful look on Jack's swollen face. He wanted to see Jack as sweet and kind, not loathsome.

Again, Atherton rescued him. "That won't be necessary. I'm putting him up until we get him sorted out."

"Well, I'll keep looking for you," Jack added. "Gimme your number. I'll call if I find anything."

"I would. If I had a phone," Morris replied. He forced an appreciative smile on his face.

When they finally outstayed their welcome, they moved back to the cruiser. Morris glanced behind him to see Cook and Jack standing sentinel by the entrance, waving him off. It occurred to him that this was the last time he'd see the Oasis, a place that did not live up to its name.

They visited the underground karaoke bar and left empty-handed. The staff said they were very sorry. His wallet and phone had disappeared, vanished in a pillar of smoke, disintegrated into dust.

They drove to the outskirts of town and into the back neighborhoods that were far more derelict than inviting. Atherton's home was a weathered bungalow with peeling gray paint and an attempt at a front garden: untamed bushes and undead flowers with patches of grass as tall as wheat. It was the kind of yard neighbors should complain over, yet the entire neighborhood looked just as shabby.

"Grab your things," Atherton said.

He led Morris across the veranda and pushed through the set of double doors opening into a dark hallway that gave the impression of coolness that wasn't quite fulfilled. The whole house stunk of potpourri; floral wallpaper cracked at its edges. Before Morris could fully absorb his surroundings, he found himself in a sitting room that was heavily draped and carpeted.

The décor was ugly but comfortable. It was full of oversized furniture that all competed against each other for space. How many could this room hold? Six at the most if comfort was an issue. He dropped his bags in the corner before sitting in a plush armchair. Around him were bookshelves stocked with mismatched ornaments, perhaps overflow from the antique shop. There were no books. There probably never were any books. The coffee table held an ornamental music box, which Atherton wound up. As it chimed, side compartments opened, holding cigarettes. "For you," Atherton said and deposited a glossy seashell ashtray next to it.

The music box summoned a handsome middle-aged woman, who appeared in the doorway. "Allow me to introduce my wife, Martha."

So, this was the wife. She was well suited to Atherton's stature, tall and strongly built, with waves of dark hair cascading down her back. Morris expected her to be stern, formal, if not suspicious of him. Instead, she exuded warmth, kissing her husband on the cheek before extending a delicate hand to Morris as if expecting him to kiss it.

"Welcome! If you get too hot, we can turn on the fans," she said. Her voice was husky, her movements dainty. She seemed completely oblivious to the large bruises on his face.

After a few moments of uncomfortable silence, Morris asked to use their phone. He needed to call home, he said. It was very important that he call home.

Martha pointed to the small side table where a rotary phone sat in a sad fashion. He balked for a moment. *Who still had a landline, much less this?* "I assume you know how to use it." She giggled to herself.

"Perhaps we could have dinner a little early tonight?" Atherton asked. "And his clothes are all dirty."

Without a word, Martha picked up the duffel bag and mentioned fresh towels in the hall bathroom in case he wanted a shower. Then she shooed Atherton out and closed the door behind them.

Alone again, Morris flipped on a desk lamp, giving an extra dose of light. A trio of porcelain dog figurines surrounded the phone, eerily hostile as if guarding it. He took a cigarette from the dispenser and lit it, sucking in the tobacco with a semblance of courage, licked his lips, then dialed Yasmin's number.

"Morris," she answered, her voice plain and determined.

"How did you know it was me?"

In the background, he could hear idle chatter, the sounds of forks clinking against plates, and light piano music dancing in the air. She was at a restaurant, no doubt, enjoying a lazy afternoon. "How could I know? Thanks to you, I've spoken with a lot of telemarketers this week." She moved outside to the backdrop of traffic, and he heard the click of her lighter followed by the exhale of smoke. "What number are you calling from?"

"It's a long story. I'm in a bind."

"Sure, you are! Does that mean you're not at the airport?"

His stomach plummeted. "No. I'm stuck, and I need help."

She cursed under her breath. "Look, we have things we need to talk about. I need to know if you're in jail or if you're in danger." He said no. "Okay, then. And since you're not at the airport, you have time to talk, right?"

"Yes. But I've had—"

"Good. Because I've been planning what I've wanted to say to you for a long time now, and at this point, I don't think I can wait for you to be here face-to-face. And I've tried waiting. I've been very patient. You may not realize it, but I have. I've called your phone for days. It only goes to voicemail. You don't answer my emails. All this time, I've sat around worrying, and I don't have anymore strength to worry about your existential crisis."

Morris was aghast. He had to remind himself to breathe. "Yasmin, please, you don't understand…"

"No, stop it. There's always something. There's always a reason or an excuse, and hard conversations never happen because of it." Her calm voice turned venomous. "You never follow through with anything. And I've waited patiently for years for you to do something. *Anything*. Not just come home. But be home and be present. Go back to school. Get a new job. Travel. Make plans for the future. And all this time, I've realized I've never demanded anything from you. I've made suggestions and have turned a blind eye every time you ignore them.

And the truth is, I've started to resent you. So much so that I've realize I'm actually relieved you're not here."

She was walking now, traversing among the sounds of honking cars and pedestrians. She did not care if others eavesdropped.

Yasmin continued. "About a year ago, I started thinking about having a baby."

His chest heightened with anxiety. "Are you pregnant?"

"No," she said flatly. "But I might be one day. I haven't decided, but I know that if I want the option, I need to be in the position to have one. And that means creating a living environment conducive to this, either on my own or with a partner." She paused again. It was Morris's turn, but he didn't take it. "I've decided that partner can't be you. I'm very sorry. I wanted to tell you this in person, but at this stage, I have no idea when that will be, and I needed to get this off my chest."

He sat there silently in the horrid little den. It was all too much. He had the sensation of being in a tight chamber that was slowly filling with water. And as the water rose, he felt the contents of the chamber rising around him, bobbing up and down, and in it was the figure of Yasmin and a baby, but also liquor bottles and the stubbed ends of cigarettes, and Henry and floating antiques, until he felt he was treading water.

"P-please…"

"Morris, stop. I'm out with friends, and I need to get back to them…"

"Please," he said again, but she spoke over him. She was preparing to hang up. "For fuck's sake, Yasmin!"

He did not mean to shout and could visualize her scowling, staring at her phone with a look of apathy, if not aggression. "Look, I know you hate me right now, but I was attacked last night, and my wallet and phone were stolen, and I'm in trouble." Silence. It was like speaking into an empty cavern, his words almost echoing back at him. "Hello? You still there?"

"What do you mean attacked?" she finally asked.

He sighed deeply. There was too much to explain. "A group of guys jumped me last night. I got beat pretty bad—my face is messed up. Still have all my teeth, so I guess that's a good thing."

"Jesus Christ, are you alright?"

"I look like shit, but I'll live. I'm at the sheriff's house. I'm safe," he said. "Last night was terrifying. I thought I was going to die."

"Did you go to the hospital?"

"No. The sheriff didn't think I needed to."

"Well, he's an idiot." She cursed under her breath. "I'm so sorry this happened to you. What do you need?"

"Come and get me?" He winced; he was asking for the impossible.

"I've been drinking," she said. Her voice was flat as still water. "I couldn't leave till the morning."

"No, I don't want you driving out here. That's ridiculous."

"Should I get you another plane ticket?"

"I don't have an ID. I couldn't get through security. But maybe you could email me a copy of my passport, even if it's expired—anything with my photo on it. I need something to prove who I am. I'll call the bank and see about getting a replacement card or something."

"Ok. Do you want me to call your family?"

He considered this: his family, the multi-headed overeager beast. His mother would take charge. She'd be on the first flight out, ready to wrap him in bells and blankets, the rest of them all assembled and awaiting her instructions. "No. The last thing I need is for them getting involved. But, if you could email my work and let them know what happened." He felt her disapproval. "It will make moving out a lot easier if I still have a job."

"Right. Consider it all done. I'll be home soon. Can I call you on this number?"

"I guess." Again, he paused. It was time, but he wasn't ready to let go. "Look, I know you're mad, and I'm sorry, but did you really mean everything you said earlier?"

"Oh, Morris. We can discuss that when you're back," she said. "But, my mind is made up. And I think when it all sinks in, you'll feel relieved, too. In the meantime, don't do anything stupid."

"I always do," he said.

The phone went silent, not because Yasmin hung up but simply because they both quit speaking. He was unaware of when he had put the receiver down but felt the urge to pull his hand back before the trio of porcelain dogs could bite him.

An odd sense of relief washed over him. He should be heartbroken, ego crumbling, but instead, he felt the weights on his chest lift; as long as Yasmin followed through, and she would, then the first steps to his rescue were in motion.

Next, he would have to call the bank, but of course, he didn't know the number. That problem was easily fixed and could wait. He leaned back into the armchair and lit another cigarette as he gazed over the den. On top of the mantel was a little brown clock, very German, with woodwork and painted figures that presumably danced about at the change of the hour. A collage of framed photos caught his eye: a wedding photo; Atherton posed in his uniform; a group of people at a barbecue; Martha in a long sundress laughing at the camera lens as if she were ready to gobble it up. There were worse places to be stranded.

During his third cigarette, Martha entered with almost psychic premonition for the downtrodden. She placed a beer in his hand and brushed the rogue strands of hair from his eyes. His clothes were in the dryer now, she said. There were towels and fresh clothes waiting for him in the washroom.

"Whenever you're ready." She smiled matronly. "We're in no rush."

The beer settled well, the shower was hot, and there was an abundance of soap scented with fruit and vanilla and other pretty smells. He soaked it all up until he felt his softness restored. Lying there on the toilet was one of Atherton's nightshirts and a pair of baggy sweatpants. He cringed at the thought of wearing someone else's clothes, but they were clean and hung off him in a comforting way. By the time he emerged, Martha had stood waiting for him in the hall.

"He wants you in for dinner," she said with the same placid smile.

He followed her into a morose dining room with wood-paneled walls and a distressed harvest table that was far too large for the three of them. Their dinner was standard fare served on mix-matched plates: strips of sautéed chicken and mushrooms, a bowl of mashed potatoes, and a side of an overcooked vegetable resembling peas. Beer bottles sat in place of water glasses, and when Morris drank his down, he didn't resist when it was replaced with another.

Both Atherton and Martha smoked steadily throughout the meal. They sat on opposite ends with their own glass ashtrays, resting their cigarettes in between mouthfuls. On occasion, Martha interrupted the silence, speaking jovially about the happenings around town, casually gossiping about her various acquaintances, while Atherton occasionally interjected with "you don't say," even though it was increasingly obvious he had no idea whom she was referring to. But it was his look, his gentle approval and soft smile, that told Morris that the two adored each other and that dinners were typically a happy time. Morris, however, felt invisible sitting there in the table's center, devouring his food by the mouthful as the beer bottles began to accumulate, and that familiar haziness drifted over him. He was trying to recall similar moments back home, in that lost time of Henry and Yasmin drunkenly rabbling around the dinette, chugging their wine and laughing over some misfortune. There had been a time when dinner was the most social part of his life.

"Morris..."

He heard his name. They were talking to him. He straightened up in his seat and refocused. Martha gave him an inquisitive look. "I'm so sorry," he said. "I have so much on my mind."

"She was asking what you do for a living," Atherton offered.

He had to think about it. "A newspaper. I do advertising," he said. "That is if I still have a job."

"Didn't you call them?" Martha asked, her eyes widening. He shrugged. "Well, tell me about your fiancé. Atherton mentioned you have a sweetheart at home."

"Sure," he said. "Yasmin is going to email me a copy of my passport, and that should help me get a new driver's license." He stumbled over his words and found that he was rambling on about the various hurdles to getting home. He took a swig of beer and winced. "May I please have some water?"

Martha returned with a large pint glass without ice. "How long have you two been together."

"Well, funny you should ask. As of today, we're not anymore." Once he said it, there was no skirting the issue. He drank down his water as if he were trying to cleanse her from his system as his hosts eyed him with raised brows. "This was going to happen," he stammered. "I think we've both known for a long time, and I should be more upset, but I'm not."

Martha reached out to pat his hand.

"You're in shock," Atherton said, lighting another cigarette.

"People change over time," Martha added. She looked

serene. Tender. "What was she like?"

"Motherly," Morris replied.

Martha smiled as Atherton opened a bottle of red wine, thick and earthy, of which he drank very little.

"Tell me about her," she said, and he described Yasmin's job at the museum, her glamorous friends and brunches, and bohemian dresses. "No. Tell me about her."

"I used to call her a free spirit, and she really hated that, but it's true. She always traveled and read these great books and knew everybody wherever she went. And then, you could spend an entire day drinking coffee with her, and you'd never run out of things to talk about. But it was always hard to know what she was thinking. I guess, by now, she's sick of me."

"Did you ever get sick of her?"

"I don't know. Maybe. I relied on her."

For dessert, there was custard and cream served in little sherry glasses. Martha proved to be a genuine hostess, full of probing questions, yet somehow was not intrusive. He settled into his dessert and wine.

Outside, the sun had set, and the temperature had cooled off. They moved to the backyard and sat around a little fire pit that illuminated the spikes of plants and overgrown weeds until it felt like a foreign wilderness. Martha lit a joint, and they took dainty drags as Morris pushed through a headrush and settled into his lawn chair, admiring the sky. The wine was sinking deep into his stomach.

They were laughing at some point at some indecipherable joke, and he was drunk off it, lapping up their laughter. Martha sat next to him closely, and he was being petted, and then there was a warm pressure against the top of his leg. The Tunnel. He hadn't realized he'd wandered in until he was deep inside. The hand crept closer toward his groin. The Tunnel was deep and ominous and poorly lit. Was it still Martha's hand? He giggled.

More laughter. More wine. And when the wine ran out, his head was spinning. "Here, take this," one of them said, and he swallowed the pill in hopes that it would steady him.

When Martha leaned forward to whisper into his ear, she was radiating light and heat, her dark hair encircled by a halo. And her lips were red, red and juicy, and bloody. He thought she was coming in to bite him, and he flinched. More laughter. This time, just Atherton, as Martha was kissing him. They were both kissing him, in turn, the odd juxtaposition of their mouths seemed impossible to decipher.

And then, he was floating, rising out of his chair, clutching the empty wine bottle for dear life, as the three of them floated together, back inside and upstairs. Atherton said something and smacked his lips. He was in his uniform one minute, and in the blink of an eye, he stood naked with the swinging pendulum between his legs. He could feel the warmth of Martha, cradling his head in her lap, her hands drifting over the buttons of his nightshirt. Cold, pinpricks of cold, clothes shed, and then Atherton's body falling on top of his to keep him warm.

"Jesus Christ! Wake him up!"

"He's fine. Let me finish..."

"But is he breathing? He's not breathing!"

"He is. He's fine. When did you become so weak?"

"I told you no more Ketamine. You always have to have things your way."

"His eyes just stirred. He's fine. You're fine."

"We haven't been fine for a long time."

"Shut up."

"At least bring him some water."

"Go get it yourself."

The room was unfamiliar. It spun out of control. He was on the spin of a pinwheel, holding on for dear life.

Then, darkness.

Chapter 13

Thirst. It was an awful nagging binding spell that Morris was all too familiar with. He felt it in his mouth, his throat, and his chest as if all parts of him had shriveled up. If he did not get water soon, the slightest touch would cause him to crumble. Strange to think that after years of hangovers and heat waves, he had never been truly acquainted with a thirst like this. He could have drunk a swimming pool, and he still would have wanted more.

It was morning. He was tangled in damp bedsheets in a modest bedroom with piecemeal furnishings. Such a simple room, the kind reserved for last-minute visitors. Underneath him, the mattress sank as if it had been punished the night before by dozens of bodies. Or just three. Now, there was only one. Steadily, he pushed himself up, moved to the ensuite washroom, and drank. Water. Life. He drank until he felt he couldn't hold anymore.

Downstairs. The house was quiet and grim; the air was so thick one could bite out a piece of it and chew. Martha sat in the kitchen, draped in an oversized kimono, bright yellow satin with a crane stitched along the side. The kitchen was a dismal, avocado green plucked from the previous century. An opened window let in the hazy light. She nodded at him and lit her Parliament.

"Up early," she said. The charm had left her and was replaced with a crusty, brittle texture. She, too, was now something entirely different. "Leaving so soon?"

"Yeah." He hadn't felt himself speak, merely heard it.

"Where?"

"Home. Hopefully."

She made a guttural, almost sickly noise before taking another drag. "How?"

The question perplexed him. He had no idea what to tell her. Even so, he didn't want to tell her anything.

"You hungry?"

No. He eyed her suspiciously. Circe had turned men into pigs with her feast simply because she could. He would not dare take another mouthful.

"There's coffee made." She pointed to the tin urn on the stove.

He managed a few sips that burned his tongue, then abandoned his cup. He needed an antidote for the previous night. It was not here. He turned away towards the front door.

"Don't forget your bags," Martha said. She lazily pointed down the hall. There was a hint of elegance in her pose, her kimono slightly open to reveal the curve of a breast, and Morris averted his eyes.

He retrieved his duffel bag and backpack, took off his borrowed clothes, and redressed out in the open. All of his movements were mechanical. The cardigan hung loosely off his body, and he wrapped it tightly around him. In the side pocket of his backpack, he found the crisp twenty-dollar bills Atherton gave him. Sixty dollars and a half-smoked pack of Parliaments. His parting gifts were so meager.

"See you around," Martha said.

"Hopefully not, but maybe," he replied.

She laughed. It was more of a quick chirp, a haughty little jab at him. And then she silently turned away in contemplation as he walked through the front door.

Overnight, autumn finally embraced the landscape with a firm grasp. Loud pops of reds and yellows graced every tree limb; the sidewalks were now partially covered with the first layer of fallen leaves that crunched under every step. Naked branches grasped out like withered claws. The chill in the air was mild; the air smelled different. By instinct, Morris followed the curved streets. He was in tune with the confusing grid of the hilly roads as if he'd always known them. He knew the difference now between the residential neighborhoods, the short squat ramblers and ranches, and the tourist streets, with their regal Victorians, and didn't shy away from a fork in the road. He walked in a daze, his steps lithe and steady, barely touching the ground. Despite this, everything felt far away.

As he approached the familiar blocks of Flood Street, storm clouds gathered overhead, casting the morning in a murky gray. A drizzle began to fall, nothing harsh, but enough to mist his hair and clothes. Usually, Morris abhorred the idea of being wet, hating the feel of soggy clothes against his skin, but he kept walking, soaking it up without a moment of hesitation.

In the distance, an elderly man sat on his covered porch. He looked like a caricature of a comic book hillbilly, complete with a white beard, oversize hat, and a plaid shirt that bulged out over his belly. Morris caught sight of him in the periphery: the man smiled and waved at him, not with urgency but with the pleasant familiarity reserved for acquaintances. It took several seconds for Morris to fully process this, and when he did, he waved back. By then, the man was looking away, enjoying the falling rain like a happy child.

The rain picked up, which made the cobblestones slick under Morris's feet and weighed down his bags, but still, he walked forward. His mind was blank. When he concentrated, he recalled the various paths necessary to reach the artist colony, the hotel, and even The Oasis. The Christ statue was up there someplace, obscured by clouds and mist, staring at him. Soon he had stopped walking, wet and breathless, and stared at the front window of Atherton's antique shop. There really was nowhere else to go.

As he stood at the entrance to the attic apartment, he could not recall the steps he had taken down the alley and up the metal staircase, nor could he explain why he had left Atherton's house in the first place. It was, by instinct, some psychological urge to return here as if he were caught in its gravitational pull. And here he was, wet with rain, staring at a closed door, one that was most likely locked. Muffled voices came from inside the apartment, and when he knocked, the door creaked open.

Henry let out a yelp, and the woman next to him turned in a defensive pose, her face combative at first but then immediately softened as her eyes traced over his wounded face.

Tina. Of all the beautiful sights to see.

"Come on in, Morris," she said as if beckoning a stray dog. He imagined crawling to her and resting his head on her chest. He felt ready to weep.

"It's all right. Come in."

Whatever trance he had wallowed in broke. He stepped inside and let his bags fall among the wreckage.

"For Christ's sake, close the door," Henry snapped. He was different now. The long matted hair and ponytail were gone, cut into an uneven crop. Even his face had blossomed, the impish boyish features restored as if he'd spent the night peeling off layers of his skin. Morris wanted to hug him. He wanted to hug both of them. He loved them so much it hurt.

"I thought you'd be long gone by now," Tina said, a hint of sadness resting behind her serene demeanor. She took Morris by the hand and led him to a chair. Her long fingers grazed his scalp and moved ever so gently down until they hovered over his injured jaw. "What happened?" she asked, though it was obvious she already knew.

"I've had a few problems," Morris said weakly. Tina stroked his arm.

"We don't have time for this," Henry said as he threw on a track jacket and pulled a large suitcase towards the door.

"Are you leaving?" Morris stammered. He felt so confused.

"It's probably best if you don't know," Tina said. "Unless you're coming, too?"

"No," Henry blurted out. "She's taking me to the bus station, and we only have one ticket."

"But I came back for you," Morris said. "I wanted to bring you home." The words sounded silly as they came out of his mouth. He hadn't, nor did he have the means to do so. They were just words, reactionary words.

Not listening, Henry continued rushing about, angrily muttering to himself. They were late; they should have left already. He pillaged shelves and boxes, grabbing little trinkets as if scared to leave something important behind. Even when he paused, he was still a pulsing ball of electricity that seemed ready to combust in a shower of nervous little stars.

Tina cleared her throat, her velvet hand still stroking Morris's arm. Her voice was calm. "Where's Atherton?" This question brought Henry to an abrupt halt.

It was so much to take in and process. He struggled to speak. "I don't know. I didn't see him this morning."

Henry cursed.

Tina moved, if not glided, to the door and stared outside. The rain faltered, and streaks of sunlight reached the stoop. "It's alright," she said. "He's either still asleep or working. There's no need to overthink this." She turned back to Morris. "If you want to help, go downstairs and open the shop. It'll buy us some time. If he shows up, say whatever you like. Henry went out for a walk. Do you understand?"

Morris quivered. Everything was happening so fast that he could barely keep up. He had only just arrived and had stumbled upon plans in mid-execution. "I'm not taking his place," he said.

"You won't." Tina kissed his forehead. "Will you help?" she asked sweetly until he nodded. Grimly. They were leaving without him. They were leaving him there. "Good. Open the shop. When Atherton stops by, tell him Henry left to run an errand, and you don't know when he'll be back. And no matter what, don't mention me. I was not here. You understand?"

"Yes." *Please don't go.* "I'll do it." *Please come back.*

"You'll be alright," she said in her serene voice.

There was an odd look on Henry's face; the jester's grin flashed and faded in one long act of resentment until there was only the shell of Henry staring at him. The cropped hair, the zipped-up jacket, and now a pair of sunglasses covering his rosy cheeks; he could be anyone now. He placed a key into Morris's hand as if bestowing him with a gift.

"Is this it?" Morris asked.

"Key works both upstairs and down. Make sure you open the curtains and flip the sign by ten," Henry said, then hesitated.

"You're welcome," Morris said with a bitter edge.

As Henry moved to the door, again he paused, giving a quick glance back over the interior. A strange gleam in his eyes as if he were mentally setting it all on fire. Then, he returned his gaze to Morris almost tenderly. "Whatever you do, don't look under my bed." He sounded like he regretted the words before he finished uttering them. But they were said, permanently carved out, and like most warnings, they made the most enticing invitation.

Before Morris could speak, Henry moved in a swift dash out the door, his feet banging against the stairwell, and there was a part of Morris that wondered if Henry would trip, fall, and break his neck. He felt it now, that light-head swirling premonition of what Henry was hiding. From the side window, he watched Henry dash across the street where Tina's sedan idled, watched him throw his suitcase into the back. And then they were off.

When people suffer a great shock, like death or the loss of a limb, they don't believe it at first. Morris thought of phantom limbs, how he would still go on feeling his fingers if he lost a hand. He would stretch them, crinkle them, make them claw at the air, all while knowing they were gone. He could not feel his hand as it reached under Henry's bed, as if the nerves had shut down, his fingers scraping against loose objects. He scooped them out in large swipes—the discarded clothes, the scattered paperbacks, empty shampoo bottles, and other debris. Among them was a small gym bag, well stashed in the depths of trash.

The bag held loose papers and receipts and spare change. And there, buried within: a wallet. It was a little brown wallet, cracked leather, that folded neatly with a green stripe. The cash was gone, but everything else was in place. The credit card, the insurance card, the driver's license with his gray-scale photo, and his name printed in small block letters: Morris Hines.

Holding it was almost painful as if every crack in the leather was razor sharp and slicing his skin with a hundred tiny cuts. Yet he clung tightly to the wallet, cradling it to his chest as if to prevent it from slipping through his fingers and disappearing again.

Bastard.

Outside, the rain picked up again; he heard its pelting against the roof and the windows. Then, his own eyes started to well up, that stinging wetness that soon progressed into sobbing. He was crying now as if his wounds had all reopened. Here the entire time within arm's reach.

You ugly bastard.

And now, he was laughing, hideous laughter. He had the keys back to his kingdom. All he needed was to make a call… His phone! Where was his phone? Another frantic search tore the bag apart and had him diving headfirst under the bed, grasping at everything. But there was nothing else but soiled clothes, empty cigarette packets, and other foul forgotten objects. Of course, Henry had his phone. Even if it couldn't be used, it could be sold.

If I see you again, I'll kill you.

Without thinking, he snatched up the little alarm clock from the bureau and threw it against the wall. It did not shatter; it would have been satisfying to watch it break. He thought of violence again, of Atherton's kind of violence: a genteel smile followed by a sucker punch to the gut. He wanted Henry harmed, physically and mentally, scarred beyond recognition. He wanted a Henry-skinned rug thrown on the floor, throat freshly slit, eyes still watering, and mouth arched open in horror.

But he was gone, gone again, and this time for good. And there was no point in wanting retribution. He now felt euphoric relief as he reopened his wallet and petted the lovely cards inside. It was time to go.

He grabbed his belongings and went downstairs, unmindful of the rain, and entered the dark antique shop. At the register, there was a phone and a large yellow book. Such things still existed in small towns like this. He called for a cab. They would be there in ten minutes, they said. And then, he felt a sudden coil in his stomach, that urge to punish, that urge to destroy. Another glance and he found the number, and before he knew it, he was calling

"Hello, Martha? Is your husband there? Is he awake? Good. I have something important to tell him."

Chapter 14

When the taxi arrived, Morris stood waiting under the spectacle awning of a Wiccan candle shop. Had the store been open, he might have popped inside and purchased some token or protective charm, anything to guarantee safe passage home. The taxi itself looked like it was in desperate need of a blessing. It was covered in dents and stuttered to a halt while making a spectrum of mechanical grinding sounds. Even the driver looked as if he were falling apart at the seams. He was a weathered man, face scarred with age as if the years had cut deeply into him. He gave a disgruntled look as Morris piled his belongings into the backseat.

"Airport, please," Morris said.

"All the way out there?" the driver stammered. His discontent was written all over his face in wrinkles.

"Yes. And please hurry."

The rain was steady now; the sky was emptying itself in a near tantrum. As the cab rolled forward, Morris leaned his head against the window and felt the steady beats of raindrops against the glass. Water, water everywhere, and not a drop to drink. He half-expected the driver to pull over and say it was too dangerous to continue. Thankfully, this did not happen. They rolled through town as he peered outward toward the blurred dimensions of buildings. Even now, the town was otherworldly, like a sunken city. It was a shame he had not experienced the better parts of it. *How did this all happen? How did I get here?* A moment later, he closed his eyes and drifted off into a meandering sleep.

He dreamt of Yasmin, draped in her printed dress, the one with the red and cream Moroccan designs, the one that hugged her curvy frame. And then, the scene shifted into him packing up his half of the apartment and her pacing around, demanding he leave one moment and bartering with him to stay the next. The scenario played out in several iterations, each more self-indulgent than the last. Finally, he envisioned an old-timey train station. He wore a long trench coat with a matching hat, very Humphrey Bogart, brooding over a glass of scotch in his compartment. As the train rolled off, Yasmin ran alongside as he stared forward.

The texture of his sleep was light and unstable, and when he opened his eyes much later, it felt like he had not slept at all. The cab came to a halt under the bleating rain, and he found himself straining to see through the fogged windows.

"We're here," the driver grunted. "Fifty dollars."

"We're here?" Morris asked. He saw nothing familiar; the terminal was either still a great distance away or obscured by the weather. Still, he fished out his credit card and handed it over.

"What the hell am I supposed to do with this?"

"What?"

"Cash only," the driver demanded.

"No. Cabs accept credit cards now. It's a thing," he said.

"Can't run it. I need cash."

He was about to argue back when he remembered the three crisp twenty-dollar bills. Atherton's money. He pulled them out, and the man greedily snatched them up as if protecting his gratuity. "Keep the change," Morris said with a grimace. As he stepped into the rain, the cab was already lolling forward as if trying to escape him.

He moved quickly to a small glass awning and glanced up at the terminal in the distance; as his eyes focused, it became clear that this was not the airport he remembered. Instead, the terminal was a small squat structure, a concrete bunker marked off by a chain link fence. Warehouses sat in the distance alongside parked aircraft, tiny ones, not the type for passengers. Through the blur, he made out the thin pavement of a runway. This wasn't an airport at all but a rundown airstrip.

And then Morris screamed. It was a gut-wrenching scream, long and breath-taking, so shrill it strained his throat. The only response was the rain bleating rhythmically against his glass shelter. Had anyone been nearby, his voice still wouldn't have reached them. And yet, the scream had a cleansing sensation; Morris felt instantly calmed, having exorcised whatever demons were in him. And now, he stared into the distance. This was only a setback; he could not be that lost. After all, this was America, the overdeveloped beast with many heads constantly trying to eat each other. It had thousands of limbs: airports, subways, cell phone towers—everything was connected. It was impossible to be that lost.

Eventually, the rain lessened, and the road became clear; Morris wasted no time in marching forward. Further down were the outlines of small boxy houses, which could have been mirages, but were still his best hope of civilization. He wrapped his cardigan tightly around him and sang songs in his head to distract himself from the biting wind. It was colder now, which only added to his determination. Among the houses, he marched. With each passing window, he glimpsed the interior lives of broken-down homes full of squalor and junk-filled living rooms, brittle furniture, ugly floral drapes, and people huddled over archaic TV sets. Otherwise, there was nothing for miles but these scattered homes, trees, and despondent road signs. *I would give up my entire kingdom for a Starbucks*, he mused.

A woman sitting on her front porch called out to him. "You'll catch pneumonia walking around like that!"

"I'm lost," he called back. "I need a phone."

"There's a restaurant up the way," she called out. "Two blocks up and to the right. But it's a haul."

He had hoped she would invite him in, maybe offer a ride or even an umbrella, but not all places held the same level of hospitality. Still, he waved his thanks and soldiered on. After endless walking, he arrived at a second stop sign, turned right, and eventually arrived at a gas station with the attached diner.

A blast of heat washed over him as he entered; the air was thick and sweltering, almost as if he had walked into a crowded sauna. The diner was full of men: men with rustic beards, thick men in flannel, men who ate pie with beer, young men who smoked and talked with the women, women who took no shit from anyone, older women with no makeup, women who drank black coffee and ate burgers with a knife and fork. No one seemed to notice him; if they did, they were too polite to say anything. He carted his bags up to a vacant spot at the counter and sheepishly signaled the waitress.

"Oh, hon, your face!" She was a freckled woman who glided up to him, coffee already poured and ready for action. "You poor thing! First cup's on me."

The dirty mug possessed a strange aftertaste that he could not identify, but he drank the coffee anyway.

"So, how you doin', hon?"

He gave her a weak, tired look until he realized she wasn't leaving without a proper response. "It's been a week," he said and forced a tired smile.

She nodded sympathetically. "Count your blessings. Could be worse."

"Order up!" The cook placed two overflowing plates on the sill, and the waitress was off.

He sat there for a while, nursing his mug. Outside, the rain continued in small bursts. Customers ordered, chatted, ate in cycles, and the waitress was hovering among them, happily chatting as she dropped off plates and checks. It was a long while before she returned to him.

"Alright, now. Whatcha having?" the waitress asked.

"Do you accept credit cards?" Morris asked.

"This ain't the Stone Age." She gave a haughty little laugh that diffused him. He ordered a fried egg sandwich and home fries.

"Betty! You got all that?"

The cook appeared in the kitchen window, scowling. "I'm not deaf!"

"But she has selective listening," the waitress said with a wink, and then she was gone again.

His food promptly arrived, and he ate it in small, measured bites, even though he wasn't very hungry. It was now a survival tactic. Best to eat while the food was available. He cleaned his plate and chugged more water. The diner was starting to thin; with a break in the rain, customers took the opportunity to pay their bills and dash out to their cars. Morris remained patient, only summoning the waitress back when she was no longer preoccupied. When it was appropriate, he inquired about a phone.

"Oh, hon, we lost the payphone years ago," she said. "Nobody used it. Everybody's got a mobile these days."

"Well, I don't," he said and ignored her quizzical look. "What about a landline? I'm trying to get to the airport, and I need a cab."

The waitress gave a little curt laugh. "Let me guess! They brought ya to the airstrip, huh? Happens more often than ya think. What time is your flight?"

"Well, I don't have one. Yet."

She nodded but then darted off, spiraling around, clearing tables, and chit-chatting with anyone amenable. He didn't blame her—it wasn't her job to take on a stranger's problems. New customers entered, and he began to worry about how long they would let him loiter at the counter. When she returned again with the same painted smile on her lips, he ordered a slice of pie to prove he was in no hurry. It came as a congealed mess on a plate, a dollop of cream melting on top; she stood there and watched him pick at it.

"So, where you from?" she asked sweetly.

"DC area," he answered and watched her eyes light up with curiosity. "I was a resident at the Manderlay Colony. You see, I'm a writer." The words felt false. He wasn't a writer, not really. He was a dreamer. He came because he dreamed of being a writer, and now he wasn't sure he'd ever write again after this.

The waitress was also a dreamer. She was suddenly lost in a fever dream, near delirious as she delved into the numerous ways her own life would make a fabulous story. How quickly she had forgotten about his predicament, that he was stranded and wounded. She looked past the ugly bruises on his face and only saw herself as the heroine of his book. How lucky was she to be in the presence of a *real writer*?

He waited patiently for her to finish, and before she could wander off again, either back to her tables or into another self-induced fantasy, he cleared his throat and interjected, "Well, the week I've had would also make an incredible story. A horror story." Again, he pressed for the use of a phone.

"Oh, hon, I'm sorry, but I can't let ya into the office. I just can't," she said. "I wouldn't mind, of course, but Betty would rat me out in a heartbeat."

"I heard that!" Betty called out again.

"Maybe I could borrow your cell phone?"

She hesitated and leaned back on her heels, creating a wide gap between them. If he lost her now, he'd lose his refuge.

Again, he willed his voice into sweetness. "I'm sorry, but I'm in a bind," he said and gestured to his wounded face. She tilted her head and nodded sympathetically, though there was still a look of skepticism. He was desperate now, desperately telling her his full story, the long version. How he'd missed his plane and lost his phone, and how in his search he was spirited away to Salvation Hill, and…

"You had a run-in with the Skeels, huh?" She leaned in conspiratorially, her face suddenly stern as if she were judging him. "I wouldn't share that with too many people 'round here," she warned. "They got far reach."

Morris nodded and glanced over his shoulder. No one had heard him. "I'm just trying to get home." And to this, the waitress nodded but was instantly called away by Betty's hollering.

Quiet. Aside from a few muffled conversations and chewing, the diner was remarkably quiet. Slowly, he became aware of the absence of background noise. No jukebox, no music streaming over speakers. Each clank of a fork against a plate was jarring. Outside, the rain was gone and had taken with it that constant drum against the windows. He fidgeted nervously. Now that the waitress knew his story, it was time to leave, but he had not paid his bill. The minutes ticked on brutally; wild thoughts crashed into his head. He was exposed here, and what if people were looking for him?

Suddenly, he became aware of a figure standing beside him—a tall, lanky man wearing a tie-dyed t-shirt, his gray hair sprouting from his head like a dustmop. The waitress took her place behind the counter, a triumphant smile creeping on her lips.

"This here is Ellis," she said. "He can take you back."

The man leaned in with a curious smile on his face. "Greetings," he said with a goofy little chuckle. "I heard you were at Manderlay."

The exchange happened so quickly that Morris flinched. He was not impressed with Ellis, the browbeaten look behind his eyes, the tangy scent on his clothes; he was probably high. Harmless, maybe, but it was still another car ride with a stranger. That, alone, unsettled him.

"I'd prefer a cab," he said.

But the waitress stood firm. "Hon, you're unlikely to get a taxi out here. This is your best shot."

"No offense, but I've been through a lot," Morris said, looking up at the stranger. "I don't know you."

Ellis shrugged with that formidable dopey expression on his face. "I get it, man. But I think you and I have something in common." He pulled up the sleeve to reveal the familiar scars along his arm, inflicted long ago, faded with years, but still raw and pink.

Morris nodded. What a shame to be comforted by someone else's wounds. "Ok then. I think I would like to ride with you," he said.

*

Ellis's car was a decrepit station wagon, baby-shit brown with ripped vinyl seating. As they approached, Morris was startled to find a large Doberman sprawled out in the back. The dog lifted its head, farted at the first sound of interruption, and then repositioned itself. *Of course*, Morris thought. In the passenger seat, his feet sunk into a layer of loose papers and carryout tins. Ellis seemed delighted to play escort. He frantically pushed unmarked cassette after unmarked cassette into the tape deck until he finally settled on the carnivalesque sounds of Blood, Sweat & Tears. *Of course.*

"So, the Manderlay Colony," Ellis asked.

Morris gave him a side-eye. "Yup."

"I love that place. I stayed there a few years ago!" Immediately, Ellis dove into a long explanation of his blobby paintings and how they represented a shapeless society. According to him, society was all a gooey mass that kept eating itself. After several tiring minutes, Morris politely suggested they get going. The dog huffed in approval.

They departed the small desolate neighborhood and moved out onto main roads, passing farmlands and cattle, until they approached the familiar signs of townships: car dealerships, budget hotels, the archways of McDonald's, and other comforts. Whatever trepidation Morris harbored started to slip away. When they reached the airport, he would go in and buy his ticket and wait in the terminal overnight if needed. There would be no more distractions or mishaps.

"Where you from again?" Ellis asked. He had spent most of the trip probing for some entry point into the conversation, and so far, Morris had deflected each one. He was in no mood to talk.

"DC," he said. "But I don't like talking politics."

"Ah. East Coast. Those parts are going to take generations to sort themselves out. Too much old money, too many migrants with nothing, and the worst politician from every state pretending they're there to keep the peace."

"Right."

"Can't tell me you're not into politics. These are scary times. We had a handle on things for a while, but it was like Pandora's box, man. All it took was one person to open that up, unleashing a lot of fury."

They continued through the winding roads. Time passed slowly, further irritated by Ellis's obsessive talking. Morris was starting the see the familiar signs of town as they moved toward the mountains. Of course, that blasted cab driver had taken him an hour in the opposite direction of the airport.

"One of the things my Aunt Bess told me, bless her soul, was that we can't let ourselves get separated. That's how they win. They separate us, and they get us suspicious of each other. It's all about unity," Ellis was saying. Or something like that. Morris had faded off. "You know what else she told me? She said 'I wouldn't trade the last twenty years of my life for the next twenty years of yours.' And you know what, I understand exactly what she was saying."

They had pulled off the main roads and were now on the winding little roads. As Ellis continued on, Morris closed his eyes, feigning sleep. *Almost to the halfway point. Then, another hour. Then home.*

"What do you think, eh?" Ellis was asking.

But Morris felt himself drifting. He was thinking of home comforts, of homecooked meals, of his friends. He wanted desperately to crawl into his own bed. He didn't bother opening his eyes. "I don't know. I think I'm just enjoying listening to you."

Ellis let out a chuckle and was quiet for several minutes. And then, the car slowed down, taking the curves easier, and Morris rose from his stupor. They were passing the familiar awnings of shops and cafes. He was sure he could glimpse the Christ statue in the distance, erected out of the sea of reddened trees, and he shuddered.

Ellis was beaming. "Where do you want to be dropped off?"

"I thought you were taking me to the airport." Morris's voice was weak.

"Airport? I thought you were at the artist colony." Ellis looked confused. "Did I mention I stayed there a while back?"

"No," Morris said. "I need to get to the airport. I'm trying to get home to DC."

The station wagon pulled into a small parking lot on the end of Flood Street, and the entrance to the Public House lurked in the distance. Tourists wandered about, many of them showing signs of day drinking.

"Oh, shit!" Ellis yelped. "What time's your flight?"

"I don't have a flight yet. But I need to get there and buy my ticket."

"Oh, man. I'm sorry. But that's another hour away."

Morris opened his mouth to speak but quickly closed it. He examined Ellis's face, carefully probing over the creases of the man's brows, the glossy emptiness in his eyes. The man looked confused as if he were mentally tracing his way back to their original conversation. But that map was probably full of its own detours and pitfalls; at any moment, Ellis might turn to him and again introduce the fact that he was a painter, that he once was a resident at the Manderlay Colony. There was no point in arguing or explaining anything. "Alright," he muttered. "Thank you for the ride, I guess."

"Well, since you still got time, why don't we grab ourselves a drink?" Ellis had regained his doltish pleasant demeanor. "I got a cabin about a mile from here. If you don't got your ticket yet, maybe we could hang out."

But Morris had already stepped out of the station wagon. He gently retrieved his duffel bag from under the poor hound, who glanced at him and snorted. "No, thank you. I appreciate the ride, but I don't want to be a bother."

"But it's no bother. I've enjoyed talking to you." Ellis emerged from the car as well. He was smiling with that ridiculous lopsided grin.

"Really, no. I think I've given up drinking."

"I'll be damned. I've taken you across the county, and you won't even let me buy you a beer? I thought we were getting along!"

Morris swallowed hard, but his patience had run dry, and the anger, once simmering embers, now reignited. "For fuck's sake, why does everyone around here get all bent out of shape if you don't want a beer? Why the fuck are you all constantly throwing booze at people you hardly know? What's wrong with you?"

Ellis responded like a startled child, tensed up with a befuddled look on his face. He really was a brittle man, all twigs and leaves, the kind that could break apart at the slightest pressure. "Wow, man. Fuck you, too." He nervously stepped back into his car, muttering incoherently to himself.

As the station wagon pulled off, Morris watched, letting his apathy roll off him. He refused to care what Ellis thought of him. *I do not owe you anything. I owe no one anything at all.*

But he couldn't just stand there all afternoon. He lugged his bags up toward the familiar territory of the park and hotel. Faces blurred around him. He paused to smoke a cigarette. With so many people out, he felt the occasional glance from some passersby and then wondered if he'd been recognized. Then, his imagination took hold and spiraled out into a perverse, if not paranoid, delusion that Scott Skeel was somewhere in the vicinity, hunting him, or that Atherton's cruiser could come drifting by at any moment and he'd be pulled inside against his will.

He stepped into a café, a pink frilly one full of lace and ribbons, the kind old ladies sat in for high tea. How silly to hide away from the main street like he was a fugitive. No one was looking for him, there was no reason to hunt him down. As the cashier called him out to him, he stepped back outside and scanned the streets. There were cars everywhere, but no taxis among them. He lit another cigarette and exhaled. *This is why they invented cigarettes*, he thought. To relax you.

At the ATM, he withdrew money and cringed when he saw the balance on his receipt. So much money was spent; his credit card was probably worse. At some point, he wouldn't be able to afford a flight home. However, a thought struck him. In his wallet was a folded piece of paper nestled among the receipts. Tina's phone number, written in blue ink. And then, he walked those same cautious steps, eyes forward, dodging the tourists. In his pocket, he fingered the edge of the antique store key. All roads seemed to lead back to the same place.

The antique store was dark, curtains still drawn, with no police cruiser in sight. One phone call and he'd be done. No more cabs if he could help it. The key slid into the lock, and the door opened, and he moved inside with only the receding light of the side windows to guide him. When he reached the counter, he stood there in the dark and dialed Tina's number.

"Atherton?" Her voice was alert, doe-like, as if on guard against predators.

"It's just me."

"Morris. How are you?"

"Did he make it?" he asked.

"I dropped him off and left. Haven't heard from him. Not sure if I will," she said. Papers shuffled. Perhaps she was at her office. "I can't help feeling a bit anxious."

He ignored the guilty swirl in his gut.

"I assume this isn't a social call."

"No," he replied. "I found my wallet. Henry had it the entire time. I bet you didn't know that." She said she didn't, and then he laughed, a quiet little self-pitying laugh, the wheezing comical laugh of idiots. He was a mess of a human being. They both knew it. "Will you please take me to the airport?"

Here he was, trying to clean up his messy self by asking another favor.

"You don't trust cabs?" she asked.

"I trust *you*. And I'd say right now you owe me."

Those were the wrong words. He knew this immediately and winced. He could feel her hesitate over the phone. This was the edge of blackmail, wasn't it? He was becoming that kind of person.

"I'm sorry. That came out wrong," he said. "I'm tired, and I'm desperate, and I can't spend another night here. Will you please take me?"

Another long pause, and he heard a deep sigh. "St. James Church. It's up the road from you. Meet me there in an hour. Would that do? It'll be dark by then. Or you can call me."

"No phone," he said. "Henry stole it."

"Well, he was desperate. We all do things when we're desperate."

"I know," he replied. "I'll see you in an hour."

He hung up.

Chapter 15

Now the Tunnel was the mouth of a snake, wide open, smiling sweetly, inviting you inside just so it could swallow you whole. It is a wonder why anyone would willingly enter. The snake always promised, "You will surely not die." Past the aperture of jaws was the long throaty staircase, poorly lit so you could only see one or two steps at a time. *Should I be here? Should I do this?* How many times have you asked yourself these questions and continued forward, knowing the consequences will be dire? To turn back now meant not knowing what awaited at the bottom. Then, there would be no story to tell.

Strange that he should think of the Tunnel now when he had long outgrown it. But as he idled there in front of the attic door, Morris sensed it all around him viscerally. *Should I be here?* he wondered.

The answer, of course, was no. The wisest decision was to leave before Atherton found him, to hike up to the church and wait for Tina. And yet, he felt compelled to come one last time. To leave too soon, to take the safe route, also had consequences. He needed to know what, if anything, lay on the other side of the door and if his actions had consequences.

At first, the door resisted him despite how the key pushed into the lock with the same ease as an unraveled thread passes through the eye of a sewing needle. Even when the lock did turn, the door held against him as if swelling into its frame. It took the full force of his body to push it open. A blast of heat, the faint taste of rust in the air. He left his bags at the entrance and waded through the unpleasantness until he stood at the precipice of the bed nook where Henry waited for him.

Poor, broken Henry. He lay naked under the thin sheet, his body sorely bruised, the deep black marks of fingers on his arms and throat, face scraped up as if he'd been dragged over gravel. There was no fight left to him, no defiant spark in his eyes, only the empty, broken shell left over.

"Did you tell him?" Henry sucked in air through the gap in his teeth.

Morris didn't respond. Instead, he dipped a hand into his pocket, touched the edge of his wallet, and rubbed a finger over the ridges of cracked leather before pulling it out and suspending it mid-air, wondering if Henry had the strength to reach out and snatch it.

"You had it the entire time," Morris said. "And my phone?"

More silence. The air was thick with it.

"Is that it? Not even going to try to explain?" Morris asked. His teeth bit his lip hard enough for the frail skin to crack. Any more pressure and it would bleed. "Do you have any idea of what you put me through? Everything I needed to get home was right here, and you said nothing. I was almost killed the other night, and then, I got stuck with Atherton, and you still said nothing." Oddly calm, his muscles relaxed as he breathed in Henry's weakness. "All for a little bit of money," Morris continued. He was trying to be the one who could see the world grandly and simply, like a ballad. "You could have just taken the cash and left everything else, you know. Hell, I would have given it to you. I would have bought you a bus ticket anywhere. And you had my life hidden under your bed the entire time and said nothing." His smile was unintentional, a cruel impulse. This was the moment he had dreamed of, the moment he had craved for so long: a confrontation where there were no escape routes or deflections, only hard truths. He waited eagerly for Henry to speak. He wanted the words to come out slowly so he could savor each one.

Henry looked away as if preserving his last bit of dignity. "Why are you still here?" he asked dangerously.

Morris felt his ego deflate. The question was there, bait on a hook, and he was disarmed by it. He began to stutter as if compelled to answer it, but *No!* It wasn't his turn to answer questions. As he realigned, he could see the blankness on Henry's face, so calm, it was gloating. Henry was mocking him now, not in words, but in silence and with his grandiose wounds and scars. And Henry lay there brightly, as bright as Lucifer before his fall, holding onto all the hard truths and swallowing them down.

"I'm... I'm leaving," he stammered. "Without you. You're going to be stuck here because of the choices you made."

"Goodbye, Morris," Henry replied and closed his eyes as if willing himself to sleep.

What happened next was difficult to remember. The world around them went black, not dark, but a pitch-black nothingness so that all Morris could see was the contours of the bed and Henry's body lying there, arms folded in peace. *Goodbye.* That word, spoken so callously, echoed from all sides.

And Morris was white-hot and radiant with the need to punish and avenge. Not just for a stolen wallet but a stolen life, entire years that were now irreversibly tarnished. He did not remember reaching for the pillow, but he held it and felt its thick puffiness in his tightly knitted fingers. Henry's face was so serene, eyes shut, mouth pursed into an evil smile. *Just do it.* Somewhere a pipe rattled and hissed. How long would it take? Two minutes? Five? It was enough time to see a week's worth of booze flow in a river, to rip apart a hotel room frantically, to feel the heat of the campfire and the steam of bubbling water, to writhe under the weight of a man he hated. He put his weight into it, pressing down on the matted pillow, and wanted to crush the entire world beneath him; there was no struggle. Slowly, gently. This is how a life is taken. And then, he was moving, not walking, but floating away, through piles of artifice, and towards the light of what could only be the very end of the Tunnel.

The world was suddenly as it should be. The evening sky grew pink; there was the honking of car horns and the damp breeze. Morris found himself back on the stoop, bags in hand, contemplating the long metal staircase and the brick-lined alley that led to Flood Street. The door to the attic apartment was ajar, and as he pulled it shut, he heard it. A laugh. One single impish laugh came and went in a single moment.

It was not a long walk across town. His eyes focused on the path ahead; his feet kept a steady pace. And yet, he could not escape the laugh. He had felt it strike his nerves as if plucking a harp. It had an impish tone, a gloating tone of triumph. Did he really hear it? Had he even entered the apartment? Or was it all a trick of the mind? There was a part of him that still hesitated, that tugged at his ankles, begging him to go back and investigate. But it was too late for that; Tina was waiting. As he walked, he tossed the keys in a nearby bin.

"Goodbye," he muttered as if he was leaving a piece of himself behind. He was different now, irreversibly changed, and was ready to let the old Morris go. Maybe, if he walked fast enough, he could outrun it. Let it stay here. Let it drift back to haunt the attic apartment and keep Henry company.

*

Tina's car was clean and smelled of mint and pine, thanks to the air freshener dangling from the rearview mirror. She drove on the back roads, broken roads of cracked pavement and loose gravel that beat against the car's underbelly in a soothing rhythm. Knifey branches hung dangerously close to power lines, and little wooded cottages blurred as they passed until they finally reached the highway and were moving steadily toward civilization. For reasons known only to her, Tina would go for the MP3 player and switch a song midway, as if she were suddenly agitated, if not offended by the current song. They moved through R&B to dance-pop to bluegrass as if she were constantly searching for appropriate getaway music.

Morris didn't mind, although he wished she focused more on the road. He sat facing away from her, staring out into the evening, occasionally hypnotized by the headlights of oncoming cars. Already the detailed images of the town were starting to fade. Once he was out of the bubble, all the glitz out of sight, the place left a dreary, bitter aftertaste on the tongue. As he thought more about the town, he could feel the musculature of his throat clench as if wanting to raise the phlegm to spit. The town was wrong; something seemed not right about the Victorian houses, gardens, and storefronts. Charming, yes, with plenty of bright colors and lights. But that only misguided you into thinking the town was kind and safe.

The drive took an hour, and they barely spoke.

She finally asked him, "You got your ticket, right?"

"I'll buy it when I get there."

"Ok-ay," she said. Then, after a suitable pause, "When are you coming back?"

He didn't look at her. "I'm never coming back."

They had sex briefly in the backseat, hidden away in the back corner of a highway rest stop. It was tight and uncomfortable, and his erection was passable, caught in a never-ending stalemate with Tina's body, feeling a short rise toward an orgasm, but neither one could finish. She laughed a little, amused by this turn of events. And Morris gave her an exasperated smile, the kind of a disgruntled teenager. Maybe he was terrible at sex or too old to accomplish the extraordinary in such cramped conditions. But the problem was more profound than that. His mind kept trailing back towards town, and when he looked at her, he was trying not to visualize the men he'd left there, the men loitering around the Oasis, how he would repaint this picture with any of them. Something had unlocked inside him; this time, it would never be fully closed.

They continued the drive, sore and dissatisfied.

Endless gas stations and shopping strips, and chain restaurants. They pulled into the parking lot of a little motor lodge close enough to see the airplanes land. Nothing was charming or quaint or remotely off about it. A simple little traveler's nook that boasted a continental breakfast and a shuttle to the airport that ran every hour.

He said, "Thank you," and Tina gave a little wave and drove off.

He booked himself the cheapest room and then, remembering his credit, called the airline and was miraculously booked on a flight the following afternoon.

For dinner, he ordered takeout from the pizzeria across the street. He bought a pack of cigarettes from the gas station and smoked two at a time. Then, he wavered over his emails. Yasmin had sent him photocopies of his passport and other documents, and there was a note from the newspaper editor that they were aware of his predicament and wished him a speedy recovery. Good old Yasmin, faithful to the very end. He thought about sending messages to other friends to check in and see who might be looking for roommates, but he didn't have the energy. That could wait until he was back and fully recovered. The rest of the evening, he watched some reality show about bored rich people arguing with each other.

It was difficult to sleep, even with the air conditioner on full blast and his pillows stacked around him like a protective barrier. Several times, Morris snapped awake with the vague feeling of danger. Like a gas leak in the motel was slowly asphyxiating everyone, or terrorists were lurking outside, waiting to break in and light the whole building up with gunfire. It was suddenly three in the morning; he was morbidly awake and restless, so we went outside to smoke. There, he stared over downtown, dead and quiet and eerily lit by the lime glow of the street lamps. He was anxious to leave such an ugly, broken-down place. Eventually, he returned to his room and hovered over the toilet, trying to piss. With one last look in the mirror, he examined his bruises, and from the right angle, they were starting to fade. Soon, they would heal. He would heal.

The following day, he awoke with heightened senses. A whiff of starch from the bed linens, the hard carpet under his bare feet, the sharp light of the bedside lamp, the frothy feel of soap. He was ready. There was no point in delaying. He checked out early and loitered in the lobby, filling up on complimentary coffee and bagels. He spoke to no one. Instead, he focused only on the clock until it was time to catch the shuttle bus. At the airport, he rushed to the ticket counter and checked his luggage, all while clutching his crisp ticket out of fear that he could misplace it at any moment.

"You know you can get those sent directly to your phone," the clerk reminded him,

Without a hint of grace, he replied with, "I know."

He passed through security with no trouble—small airports have short lines—and soon, he stood in front of his gate with over an hour to spare before his flight boarded. There was a small restaurant and bar down the terminal, and for a moment, he felt tempted to go in and order a beer. Something light, something to make him brave for the flight home. But then, he shook his head with temperance.

"I will never drink again," he muttered. "Except in good company."

That was when the anxiety rose. In that final hour, he kept glancing over his shoulder, half expecting some uniformed menace to come for him. Everywhere he looked, strangers represented hidden dangers, and security cameras focused on his movements around the terminal. When they called his boarding number, he kept his head down as he stepped in line and could barely breathe until his ticket was scanned and he was boarding the plane. But even then, in those terrible moments waiting for takeoff, while the flight attendants moved through their usual rounds and gave their safety instructions, he sat there clutching his armrest in painful suspense. He was waiting for it, that moment when he would hear his name suddenly called over the speakers, and with the push of a button, his seat would drop out from underneath him, sending him down a long metal chute and into the clutches of Atherton, who could cart him back to town and to whatever judgment awaited him.

Author's Note and Acknowledgements

It all started with a place.

The first time I visited Eureka Springs was in 2012, when I accepted my first residency at the Writer's Colony at Dairy Hollow, and I was instantly enchanted. I loved being at a writer's colony. I love the quiet days in my studio, plenty of time to think and feel and write. I also loved being in this little artsy town in the Ozarks. There was something magical about the place, some indescribable quality that was very bohemian and very queer. By the end of that first trip, I didn't want to leave.

For over a decade, my trips to Eureka Springs have become a yearly tradition and now it feels like a home away from home. Even as I type these words, I am flooded with memories, far too many to list: those evenings spent on the patio of Brews or in the scotch bar of the Rogue's Manor; buying tin art from the fabulous Sue Moore-Glave (now deceased); random memories of ghost tours and art shows and heart-to-heart talks with strangers. I have made such amazing friendships there. I know I'm only a yearly visitor who drops in for a few weeks and disappears, but I think of them all year in anticipation of our next reunion.

I started writing this book shortly after my short story collection was published. I was in my studio at Dairy Hollow, staring a blank screen, with this vague idea of a modern man who becomes stranded in middle America. Once the thought took hold, I could only see the town around me and what it must look like through his eyes.

It's possible to love a place with the same intensity you would a person. It becomes a part of you, woven into your psyche. You share a history. You learn its secrets. And there is a sense of loss when something changes. When I started this book, I knew I couldn't set it in Eureka Springs. It felt against the rules, like I was breaking trust.

Writers should never be trusted.

You Don't Belong Here is set in an unnamed town whose location is purposefully left ill-defined. The characters within should not be confused with anyone living or dead. Some of the landmarks will be familiar to those who know where to look, but I assure you, they are not the same. One day, when I'm ready, I'll write that essay about my relationship with Eureka Springs and its people. There will be no need to make it dark or dramatic. I will paint that picture as I've always known it, with love and admiration.

In the meantime, I want to thank the town of Eureka Springs and all my wonderful friends for sharing your home with me. Special thanks to the Writer's Colony at Dairy Hollow for giving me a space to do what I love most, especially to Linda Caldwell, Jana Jones, and Michelle Hastings Hannon.

Much love and appreciation to Steve Berman: publisher, editor, and friend. Seriously, I owe you so much for helping me bring this book to life.

Much gratitude to my many friends and colleagues for your continued support of my quirky ambitions. Thank you to Angela Brown for her editorial expertise, as well as Arielle Bernstein, Dan Brewer, Jeffrey Luscombe, Jolie Mandelbaum, and Melissa Wyse, who each gave generous feedback. To the amazing Stephanie Grant, thank you for your advice and kindness, as well as to Nicholas Benton and Philip Clark for all the pep talks. To Leet Wood, who joined me at Dairy Hollow one summer, and sat up all night with me while I stressed over the novel's ending – I'm so glad we got to share that experience.

Lastly, thank you for my wonderful husband, Gordon. At the end of the day, you are always the home I return to.

About the Author

Jonathan Harper is the author of the short story collection *Daydreamers*, a Kirkus Review's Indie Book of the Year for 2015. His writing can be found in numerous places like *The Rumpus, The Rappahannock Review, The Dillydoun Review, Chelsea Station*, and in numerous anthologies including *Homewrecker: an Adultery Reader* and the *Best Gay Stories* series. He received his MFA from American University and currently lives in Northern Virginia.

CPSIA information can be obtained
at www.ICGtesting.com
Printed in the USA
JSHW020840230523
42098JS00001B/26